THE STREETS NEVER LET GO 3

Lock Down Publications and Ca$h Presents
THE STREETS NEVER LET GO 3
A Novel by *Robert Baptiste*

Lock Down Publications
Po Box 944
Stockbridge, Ga 30281

Visit our website @
www.lockdownpublications.com

Copyright 2023 by Robert Baptiste
The Streets Never Let Go 3

All rights reserved. No part of this book may be reproduced in any form or by electronic or mechanical means, including information storage and retrieval systems without permission in writing from the publisher, except by a reviewer who may quote brief passages in review.
First Edition January 2023
Printed in the United States of America

This is a work of fiction. Names, characters, places, and incidents either are products of the author's imagination or are used fictitiously. Any similarity to actual events or locales or persons, living or dead, is entirely coincidental.

Lock Down Publications
Like our page on Facebook: Lock Down Publications @
www.facebook.com/lockdownpublications.ldp

Book interior design by: **Shawn Walker**
Edited by: **Nuel Uyi**

Robert Baptiste

Stay Connected with Us!

Text **LOCKDOWN** to 22828 to stay up-to-date with new releases, sneak peaks, contests and more...
Thank you.

Submission Guideline.

Submit the first three chapters of your completed manuscript to ldpsubmissions@gmail.com, subject line: Your book's title. The manuscript must be in a .doc file and sent as an attachment. Document should be in Times New Roman, double spaced and in size 12 font. Also, provide your synopsis and full contact information. If sending multiple submissions, they must each be in a separate email.

Have a story but no way to send it electronically? You can still submit to LDP/Ca$h Presents. Send in the first three chapters, written or typed, of your completed manuscript to:

LDP: Submissions Dept
Po Box 944
Stockbridge, Ga 30281

DO NOT send original manuscript. Must be a duplicate.

Provide your synopsis and a cover letter containing your full contact information.

Thanks for considering LDP and Ca$h Presents.

Robert Baptiste

Chapter One
Soulja Slim
Years Later
2002 February

It was 12:01. I just got released from prison. I was standing outside of Allen State Prison which was up North Louisiana, smoking a cigarette and waiting on my girl; she came to pick me up. As I smoked on my cigarette, I thought about my dawg and who killed him. Word on the streets was this bitch Michelle Uncle—Peter—killed him. He ran down on him in the Melpomene Projects while he was arguing with that bitch, and shot him twice in the head. He never saw it coming. People say they didn't know he was going to kill him, but I know that was a fucking lie. My city is so cut-throat to the bone. You can't trust nobody. The bitch probably had something to do with it. As a matter of fact, that was why I was thinking about calling my record label *Cut-throat Committed.*

My girl pulled up in front me in a red G-Wagon with chrome and tinted windows. She stepped out looking good wearing pink leggings that showed off every curve, even had her pussy print out. She had the matching halter top that held her round nice size titties in place and her hard nipples poking out. Her long black hair hung down past her shoulders, and her red lips stick had her lips looking good. Her nails and pretty toes were polished red and were hanging out of some white and pink Chanel sandals. She had my dick palpitating from how good she looked. I couldn't wait to get home to eat and fuck the shit out of her.

She walked up to me, hugging and tongue-kissing me. She smelled so good I wanted to eat her right in the car. I'm not going to lie I got a good girl. No matter what I gothrough, she's always there. I need to think about chilling out in them streets and get my shit together for her. I gotta think about settling down and taking this music shit serious, then have a few kids and get married. You know, turn in my player card. Because Kim has been rolling with me for years and never felt off.

"I see you happy to see me." She smiled, pressing up against my dick.

"You already know." I smiled.

"Love you."

"Love you back."

We made it back to the city in three hours. When we hit her bedroom door at her apartment in Slidell, she went to take off all her clothes. I just watched her for a minute as she took off her clothes. Kim's body was looking right. She told me she was working out at the gym while I was gone. Damn! She looked good. I watched as her pretty red titties set up like missiles, with her pink hard nipples pointing straight at me. Then she stepped out her leggings with nothing on underneath and her pussy well shaved. I wanted to jump on her. She laid back in the bed, spreading her legs.

"Come here," she said, smiling, licking her lips.

I dropped my clothes to the floor, showing her my long, hard, black dick. I pulled her to the edge of the bed, getting on my knees, eating her out. I licked her from her pussy to her asshole. She moaned all the way.

"Yes, baby, don't stop! I'm fucking coming." She held my head down, coming back to back in my face.

I raised up. She crawled toward me, putting my dick in her mouth, sucking on it. She deep-throated my dick and sucked on my balls until I came. She pulled back, laid back on the bed as I climbed on top of her. I put her legs on my shoulders as I slid my dick deeper in her tight and soaking wet pussy wall.

"Fuck! I love you, Morris," she said, digging her nails in my back, as I stroked her hard and deep.

"Damn! This pussy is good, Kim," I said, going even deeper.

"I'm about to come again," she said, with her whole body shaking.

I flipped her over, grabbed her shoulders, slamming my dick into her from the back as she called out my name.

"Fuck! Slim, give me that dick, it feels so good."

I slapped her on the ass and pulled her hair as she gripped the sheet, coming back to back and screaming out my name.

"Slim! Slim!" She went to fucking me back as I thrust in and out of her.

"I'm about to go nuts, Kim!"

"Yes, daddy, shoot that nut all in this pussy."

I held her ass cheeks tight as I came in her pussy, while she came all over my dick. We laid there for a couple minutes with my dick still hard, trying to catch our breath. A few minutes later, we were back at it, fucking like dogs.

Robert Baptiste

Chapter Two
Soulja

I got up the next morning feeling good. I was free. I got in the tub and soaked for a minute. It felt good to take a nice hot bath. I soaked for thirty minutes. I dried off and walked back to the bedroom. I went to the closet. Kim had brought me all kind of new clothes and outfits. I grabbed some blue Girbaud jeans, all-white Polo shirt, a black wife-beater, and threw it on along with some fresh black Soulja Reeboks.

I smelled the breakfast Kim was cooking from the kitchen. I walked in the kitchen. Kim had on my *Saints* t-shirt, standing over the stove, cooking some grits. I walked over, kissing her on the neck and rubbing her on the ass.

"Hey, baby," I said.
"Good morning, love."
"Baby, where's my money?"
"Hold on, nigga, eat first," she said, fixing me some food.

She had made cheese grits, bacon, eggs, and orange juice. She came back in the kitchen with a black bag. I opened it up, and it looked light.

"Kim, this is not two hundred and fifty thousand dollars."
"I know. It's a hundred and fifty thousand dollars."
"Damn! Kim."
"Well, I had to pay lawyer fee, bills, take care of your ass in jail, and *treat* myself to something. I needed to shop some toys—they took care of my sex urges while you were gone."
"You should have gotten some dick."
"Baby, stop."
"Did the label send the check?"
"Yes."
"How much?"
"Two hundred thousand."
"Damn! My album mustn't do shit."
"They said it sold two hundred thousand copies."
"Damn! That ain't shit on a nationwide label."

"No promotion. Your ass was in prison. Baby, you got the talent. You need to start taking this shit seriously," she said, sitting on my lap.

"I know."

"So what are you going to do now?"

"I was thinking about starting my own shit."

"You need to since the record company dropped you."

"You're right. But I'm going to need more than this bread."

"You figure it out. You always do. I got your back. Meanwhile, I need you to get the paperwork moving and the rest of the shit that goes with starting a label."

"A'ight."

"What are you going to call it?"

"*Cut-throat Committed.*"

"I like that."

"But first I need something to ride in. I need to get me a true whip."

"Okay. I'm going to bring you to the dealership. Where you trying?"

"I want that new 2002 Cadillac truck I was seeing on the TV commercial."

"Okay. It cost around eighty thousand dollars."

***

We walked on the Cadillac dealership parking lot. I spotted the truck I want off the back. It was all-black with schrome factory rims and tints on it. It was a black Escalade. I walked over to the truck, trying to see through the window. Just then, a slim black woman came out wearing a purple dress, and heels to match, with her black hair hanging to her shoulders.

"Yes, can I help you?" She smiled.

"Yea, this truck I want."

"Okay, fully loaded, it costs seventy-five thousand dollars."

"A'ight. I'll take it."

It took us about an hour to fill out all the paperwork. I give her $75,000 cash money. I don't have time for no car note, fuck that shit.

"Look, keep the check in the bank. For a hard time. I'ma take this fifty thousand dollars and make something happen. You know—start getting that label paper started."

"I got you. Be safe."

"Love you," I said, kissing her. "Love you more." Fresh out of prison, I pulled off the Cadillac parking lot with a sleek 2002 Escalade. I rode around the city, checking it out as I smoked on a camel hump cigarette, wanting to smoke some weed. As I pulled into the gas station on Claiborne to get me a Cigar, I thought I saw Sharon getting gas. I stepped out of the truck, and it was her. She was getting some gas. She had on a white dress and pink ballet flats. She looked like she was pregnant.

"Hey, Slim!" she said.

I walked over toward her to see if she was pregnant. And, sure enough, she was really pregnant. I was fucked up in the head that she moved on so quick. Hoes ain't shit. I just looked at her as she walked over to me.

"What's up, Slim? You're not going to give me a hug?"

"Nothing. Coolin."

"Kim told me you got out."

"Yea, yesterday."

"Why are you looking at me like that?"

"Shit! I can't believe you're pregnant and moved on already?"

"What I'm not supposed to do?"

"Shit! I thought for at least two years."

"You sound like I don't love Tre or something?"

"Shit, did you?"

"Slim, you got the nerve to ask me that? I stood down with Tre through thick and thin!" she said, with tears coming down her face. "I still love him. When that nigga died, it broke me in half. I wanted to kill myself. The only thing that kept me alive was our son. I know I had to live for him. Yea, I met somebody else, moved on, got pregnant, and I'm about to get married to a good man. But I will never forget Tre. You and everybody else can kiss my ass."

"I hear you."

"Look, I need you to follow me home. I got something to give you."

"Okay."

We pulled up to a big red brick house. She went inside and came back out a couple seconds later with a big black bag.

"Here. I took the money. But I'm sure you can do something with this."

I opened the bag, and it had two bricks of heroin. "Okay. You are easy," I said, pulling off.

Upon my arrival home, I walked inside. Kim was watching TV. "What's wrong, baby?" she asked.

"Nothing," I said, going to the bedroom.

She followed me. "Something is wrong."

"I'm cool."

"Good because I been thinking about moving out town, you know, getting a fresh start. What do you think about that?"

"I'm not going anywhere. You can go. If you want to."

"Damn! Slim, what's wrong with your ass!"

"I saw Sharon ass at the gas station, pregnant. It fucked me up."

"Yea, she moved on."

"I see."

"Yea, what you thought she was going to do? It's been a year and a half."

"I guess I'm only feeling the pain from my best friend."

"Not everybody just moved on from it. But you need to do."

"Never going to do that."

"You need to."

"Shit, you lucky I came out."

"You need to let that go. Tre is dead."

"Would you let it go if it was your best friend?"

"I'm just saying."

"Kim, how are you going to tell me how to feel? My best friend is gone and I wasn't there to help him. He is gone and never coming back."

"Slim, I'm not trying to tell you how to feel. But I'ma tell you that you can't expect people to stay stagnated and put their life on hold.

It's sad but that's the kind of lifestyle y'all living."

"I'm not going to listen to this shit!" I said, going upstairs. I lay in the bed with my head and heart hurting, feeling fucked up about my dog, knowing Kim was right. But I'm not giving up. I'm going to kill everything that had something with my nigga death. A couple hours later, Kim walked into the room. She slid into the bed, laying her head on my chest. I started rubbing my hands through her head.

"Babe, I'm sorry about today. And what I said."

"Babe, you don't have to be sorry about speaking your mind and how you felt. I still love you."

"And I love you back."

***

Soulja

I pulled up to my mother's house in Bunker Hill. Niggas were hustling all in front of her house. I need to buy my mother a house and move her from around here. Because it's just like living in a project around this motherfucker. They do everything niggas in the projects do around here. I walked up to her door, knocking on it.

"Who is it?" she asked.

"Me."

She opened the door.

"Hey, baby," she said, hugging me and kissing me on the cheek.

I'm glad you're home."

"Me too."

"Come on in."

She had some Gumbo cooking.

"You want something to eat?"

"Hell yea." I sat at the kitchen table while she fixed me a plate of Shrimp Gumbo.

"So what are you going to do with your life, Slim? I'm tired of you going in and out of prison."

"Me too. I'm getting tired."

"What if you settle down with Kim and have some kids?"

"I've been thinking about it. But first I'm going to try and get this label off the ground."

"I'm sorry about your friend Tre."

"It's cool. The nigga going to pay."

"Slim, you need to leave it."

"Mom, you know that is not going to happen."

"Well, okay, I'm going to pray for you."

"No, pray for that nigga when I catch him."

"My child, what am I going to do with you!"

"Well, I'm going to start my own label and make some money so I come buy you a house."

"That sure would be nice. But I want you to get out them streets and do something with your life. That's what will make me happy."

"I got to go, mom," I said, kissing her on the cheeks.

"So soon. Stay a lil' while."

"Okay. When was the last time you talked to my brother?"

"A couple days ago."

Just then her phone rang. "Hello."

"Hey, mom."

"I'm glad you called. Your brother's right here."

"What's up, nigga?" my brother said after our mom handed me the phone.

"I'm coolin'. Just got out."

"I see. I'm sorry about your friend."

"I'm cool because the nigga going to be there with him when I catch the bastard."

"Man, you need to chill in these streets."

"Yes. I'll, after I get this nigga."

"I hear you."

"You need some money? I'm going to shoot you two grand. I'm going to give it to our mother."

"Okay. Love you, bro. Stay safe."

"A'ight. I got this."

"Later."

I gave my mother two grand for my brother, kissed her the cheeks, and dipped.

Chapter Three
Kim

I got up the next morning feeling for Slim. He was gone. I know Slim wasn't going to change who he is. And I know damn sure he wasn't going to move out of town. He got to be where all the drama was. This is how he came up. He's a real street nigga, and that's what attracted me to him. His thug out way, dope dick, tattoos, gun carrying, robbing and killing niggas. Plus going in and out of prison. That's him. Do I get tired of the shit? Yes, I do. But then it's all part of him and what I signed up for. He is really Magnolia Slim. New Orleans' fineness—the heart of the street with a big dick that I love. So it would be crazy of me to try and change him.

The people love him because he keeps it all the way street and real. That is why they buy and love his music. Because he speaks the truth. So I got to let him do him. I just got to put more life insurance on him and pray to god to keep him safe.

I heard the water running. I got out of bed and joined him in the shower. I wrapped my arms around his waist.

"Hey, baby, I love you," I said.

He turned around and kissed me. "I love you back."

"Whatever you want to do, I'm with you."

"A'ight. I got to go and visit my friend's grave."

"Okay."

He picked me up, slid his dick in me, then I bounced up and down upon him as he made love to me.

Robert Baptiste

Chapter Four
Len

I was lying across the bed in my blue boy shorts, pussy on fire, needing some dick. The nigga I was fucking with out the Melp just got locked up. I wasn't with joshing no nigga, so I let his ass go. I wish the nigga was here right now to put this fire out. I put the blunt out. As I was leaning in my drawer to get my silver bullet, my phone rang. l looked at the number. I know this wasn't who I thought it was. I picked up the phone and answered. "Nigga, what's up? You finally decide to call a bitch."
"Yea, I know. I just got out."
"When?"
"A day ago.
"Where are you now?"
"I just left Tre's grave. I'm on the way to the project."
"Okay. Give me a minute."
"A'ight."
I jumped up, went and jumped in the shower, shaved my pussy, and washed my body. I got out and sprayed Chanel perfume on my body and inner thighs. I put on a sundress with no panties. It was hot out. In the middle of June, the sun was fucking smoldering. I pulled my hair back in a ponytail and slid on some Gucci sandals. I grabbed the blunt and my keys and headed out the door. I stood in the driveway for about five minutes. Then he pulled up in a black Cadillac truck with a dark-tinted window. He stepped out looking good to me. I walked up to him, hugging and kissing him.
"Nigga, I miss you."
"I miss you too."
"How was it in the A?"
"That shit wasn't for me."
"I know you weren't going to make it there. You New Orleans Magnolia."
"Yeah. Look, what's up with my project?"
"Ain't nobody been in there."

"Cool. I got a couple bricks of heroin."

"Shit, I'm glad you're back. I need two things from you: dick and money."

"What has been dry back chere?"

"Rell got some dope. But that bunk. Fiends been going elsewhere. The project ain't been popping."

"Okay, let me put this up."

"I'll put it in my house," she said, grabbing the bag, and running upstairs to her apartment."

We jumped in the truck and pulled off.

As we were riding around the city, she went on to lace me on a lot of shit in the street.

"Word on the street is, that bitch Uncle killed Tre because y'all robbed and killed his brother."

"She set him up."

"That is not the word on the street. They don't know."

"Where the bitch stays?"

"Somewhere in Kenner. She is a stripper now. She got Tre baby."

"A'ight. I'm going to find that nigga and that bitch."

"Just be careful. You still got money on your head."

"Yea, I know this beef shit won't stop. Who got the money?"

"The nigga out the eight ward—for shooting up them people. Some nigga I forgot his name. Them niggas out the 17th been coming back here looking for you."

"Favor probably."

"I don't know."

We pulled up to the daiquiri shop.

As we ordered our daiquiri, she was still lacing me on shit.

"What's up in the projects for real?"

"Them nigga beefing with everybody. Calliope, 3 and G, Melp, the whole city. A lot of them niggas came home on that jacking shit. Old man Leslie too is home."

We jumped back in the truck.

"Yea, when he came home?"

"Shit, a couple months ago. Robbing shit. He got the beef going on with the Calliope. He killed Jack Ruff and put him in the dumper.

In the seventh ward."

"Damn! Shit wild out."

"Yes, every day somebody comes back there shooting shit up."

"Okay. Who got the dope back there?"

"Stone had it but he just got busted by the feds a couple months ago."

"Damn! The feds back there like that."

"Yea, with all that shooting and killing, plus a little kid got shot the other day back chere."

"Damn! So what you got going on? What nigga you fucking with?"

"I was fucking with this nigga out the Melp. But his ass went to jail a couple months back."

"You like them nigga out the Melp?"

"Whatever, nigga. Pull up to the telly so I can get some of that dick."

"Like that, huh?"

"Nigga, my pussy on fire. I haven't had dick in six months."

As soon as we hit the telly door, he had me bent over on the bed, slamming his big horse dick in me and slamming me on the ass.

"Fuck this pussy, nigga! I miss that dick."

"Fuck! That pussy is good," he said, slamming me on the ass. I looked back at him, sweating, biting on my bottom lip, my body shaking.

"Fuck! Nigga, I'm coming," I said, shaking on that dick. He flipped me over with my legs on his shoulders and fucked the shit out of me like DMX did Keisha on *Belly*. I was coming out of every hole in my body, loving it.

"I'm about to come," he said, shaking.

I wrapped my legs around him as he shot his nut all in me.

"Fuck!" he said, laying his sweaty body on top of mine as we caught our breath.

***

Soulja

I dropped Len off in the project and headed to the parkway, hoping to catch up with that nigga Mike. I need to come up with a couple beats for this new album I got in mind. I'm trying to set the streets on fire with this one. Fuck a major deal. I need all my money. After this, I'm going legal and getting the fuck out of New Orleans. Now it's time to fall back and chill.

I pulled up on the parkway; them niggas were out pushing work getting their hustle on. I stepped out of the truck. All them niggas came up giving me daps.

"Soulja, when you got out?" Dre said.

"A couple of hours ago."

"Man, we got the camera rolling, doing the new exposé of the underground rappers in New Orleans."

"Oh yea. Stop out to everybody. Real nigga Soulja Slim holding it down for the city like a big dog. Watch out for my CD coming to you soon. It's going to set the world on fire. You understand me?"

"Yeah, good looking out," Warren said.

"Look, I got that fire dope."

"Cool. We need some around here. They got bunk shit!" Dre said.

"Holla at me, baby. Mike home?"

"Yea, that nigga in there."

"Later."

I walked up to the house. The first thing I heard was a fire beat coming from the studio. I walked in, and his ass was sitting with another young black producer.

"Slim nigga, when you got out?" he said, hugging and dapping.

"Not too long ago."

"Man, I was just telling Daniel here how I wish you was out here."

"Yea, I feel you."

"What up, Soulja?" Daniel—the young black producer—said. I nodded at him.

"Look, nigga, I just dropped by to tell you I need some fire beats for this album I'm dropping. On my own shit."

"What is your label called?" Daniel asked.

"Cut-throat Committed."
"I like that."
"Okay. You got some beats for me?"
"Yea, I got a bunch shit at my house."
"Okay, hit me up."
"Got you."
"Where you stay?"
"On the 13th of Valence and Magnolia."
"Okay."
"I'm working with the younger BG."
"Okay, I fuck with family music."
"Cool, I'm going to shoot the info later."
"A'ight, bet."

I stayed for a few minutes and listened to some beats. After a while, I told them I was leaving. Then I went back in the truck, lite me a blunt, and smashed out to the project.

I walked into my project apartment and turned on the window unit because it was hot as a motherfucker here. I sat back on the couch, snorting a bag of dope and popping a few pills. I laid back, enjoying my high. I woke up a few hours later to a knock at the door, and my phone rang. I picked the phone up and answered the door.

"Hello?" I said.
"I was checking on you. I haven't heard from you," Kim said.
"My bad. I was caught up on something."
"You thinking you come home after I get off from work and we can finish what we started last night?"
"All for it, love you."
"Love you more."

Len was at the door.
"What's up, Len?"
"I need money to get the stuff to cut and bag this shit up."
"A'ight."
I handed her a 100-dollar bill.
"I need my change back."
"Boy, whatever."

A few hours later, I had a hold of a brick of dope on her table. We were mixing up with the mannitol. I was going to make a brick in and half out this one. I need to make a million dollars so I could start this label off. I needed to get my studio time, promotion time, and beats. And that shit not easy.

"Look, I need to make a million off this shit."

"That shouldn't be a problem with all that bullshit dope back chere. Few niggas got some back chere on the other side. But not in the circle. That shit nothing."

"Good 'cause after I sell these keys, I'm out.

"Where are you going?"

"Flying straight trying to get me a deal. And take this rap shit serious, and get my mother a house. And try to have a family."

"I heard that. I hope it works out for you and Kim."

"That's what's up."

"You know I'm lying, right?"

"Whatever."

We finished bagging up the dope. I took a couple bags out with me like always, passing them out. Before you know it, I had a motherfucker lineup copping dope.

Chapter Five
Soulja

When I pulled up in the project, Rell and Craig were standing in the courtway, talking and smoking.
"What's up with you niggas?" I said, dapping them off.
"Slim, nigga, what good? You back, huh?"
"Nigga, you know I'm Magnolia to the bone."
"Nigga, what's up?" Craig said.
"Shit! You know this shit doesn't stop with me. From the pen to the grave is what it is."
"I feel that," Craig said.
"What's up with this motherfucker that killed my dawg?" I asked.
"I'm on it. I told that nigga don't go by that hoe but that nigga didn't want to listen to me," Craig said.
"I know the nigga hardhead," I said.
"For sure."
"Look, you niggas need to give me a gun," I said.
"Man, I got you," Rell said.
I followed him upstairs to his bitch apartment. We went to the back left, up the mattress. They had all kinds of guns under there.
"Damn, nigga, you at war?"
"Nigga, you got stay heated. With all the beef going on back here."
"Feel you."
"I don't know what you are going to need."
"At least I'm not the only nigga back here beefin'."
"You're right about that shit. Niggas not getting money back here no more."
"Yea, selling that bunk ass dope. People don't want that shit."
"Nigga, I got some fire."
"Nigga, put me down."
"I got you."
"A'ight, I need to get some money."

"A'ight. Look, give me that .45, and the 9mm with the extended clip, and that chopper."

"Okay. Nigga, you owe me."

"I got you."

I brought the guns to my apartment.

Rell, Craig, and I walked into Len's house; she was in the kitchen breaking down a 4 half dope. As for the dope, I could take a seven, but I was going to put a three on it and make a half brick out of it.

"Hey, baby," Len said, getting up, and kissing me. "What's up, Rell?"

"Nothing, cool," Rell replied. We all took our seats, and I proceeded to lay things bare to Rell and Craig about my plans. "Man, look, I got some dope. We going to bring the money back to the projects. Plus I'm about to start this Cut-throat Committed Label. Can you niggas handle the dope trade?"

"We can do that," Rell and Craig said in chorus.

"Okay, this is our team. I'm going to supply y'all with the dope."

"It's all love."

We sat there mixing and cutting up dope. I turned the 4 half into a half brick.

A few hours later, we had the circle bumping with that fire dope. Niggas, bitches, and dope fiends were coming from all over to cop them twenty-dollar bags. I had the biggest and raw dope in the city. A dope fiend came up to me and told me somebody O.D'd in the hallway off that dope. Now this shit really about be jumping, because the dope fiends want what just killed that nigga. And the jack boys going to be around trying to see who got keys to dope. So, now my crew and I got to be on point. Because a nigga will come in the project and try to catch you slipping and rob you.

Chapter Six
Soulja

The next day I pulled up in Oakwood Mall parking lot to get me some clothes and tennis shoes. As I was parking my truck, I saw this fine ass woman with a round ass bending over in her car, wearing some blue leggings with a halter top to match. *Damn, this bitch fine. I got to holla at her. I need some new pussy on my team*, I thought to myself. I stepped out of the truck and walked over to her.

"Excuse me. Do you need some help?"

"No, I got it," she said, turning around, and smiling.

I knew her face but I forgot her name, and I don't think she was this thick. She was the chick I had met at the second line, but never got around to fucking her.

"Boy, Slim, what's up?" she said, hugging me.

"What's up, love?" I hugged her back. She smelled so good.

"You don't even remember me."

"Yea, I do, from the second line. But I forgot your name."

"Dayton."

"Yea, don't you feel like hell!"

"I couldn't be too fine. You ain't holla."

"Well, shit, I had a lot going on in my life. You know how these streets are. I just came home from jail."

"Oh, really?"

"Yea, had to go do a year and six on a violation."

"Okay, so where are you going?"

"I'm about to go to the mall."

"Me too."

We walked into the mall, shopping and talking. I bought me some Girbauds, Polos, and Reeboks. I even brought her a thong and bra set from *Victoria's Secret*.

We sat in the food court, talking and eating.

"So you got a girlfriend?"

"Yeah, but she doesn't stay in the city."

"Oh, where is she staying?"

"In Atl. You got a nigga?"

"No, niggas don't want no bitch for a woman. You know how that goes. Every stripper fucking and sucking."

"I'm knocking you to get your money."

"I hear that."

"I'm saying you got to get how you get it."

"At least you're real."

"I walked it like I was living it. You ain't listen to my music. That how I'm living. I ain't no stunt. Real to the bone."

"So you come out with some music."

"Yea, as soon as I get my money up. Starting my label. *Cutthroat Committed*."

"That's good. Because I was just about to ask you where you're going now that you're out."

"I'ma do what I've been doing—hustling, snort dope, smoking blunts and fucking hoes, and holding it down for the Magnolia."

"Well, put me on the list to get fucked."

"Like that."

"Ain't had any in two years. After my boyfriend got killed."

"You got kids?"

"No."

"Where you stay?"

"In Kenner."

"Here, my number. Hit a nigga up."

"I got you, love," she said, smiling, getting up.

I watched as she walked off, putting some more twists in her hips because she knew I was watching.

***

After I left the mall, I headed to Daniel's house in the 13th ward. He had hit me up while in the mall, telling me he had some new tracks for me to listen to.

I pulled up on the 13th on Valence and Magnolia, where this nigga BG live and rep. I like him; he's a cool nigga. A real street nigga. He trying to do his own thing since he left the label. I hit the blunt, stepped out the truck, and grabbed my pad. I got a lot of rappers from jail on it. I walked up to the door and heard a sound coming from it. I knocked on it. Daniel opened the door, smoking a blunt.

"Come on, nigga. We just dropped a live track."

"What's up?" I said, dapping him off.

"Come with me."

We walked down the stairs to his base where he had the whole hook up. He had booths, the beat machine, and all the stuff you need to make a hit.

"What's up, Slim?" BG said.

"Nothing, cool."

He dapped it off. Then I sat down and listened to some beats. "What are you working on?" BG asked.

"Some new shit for my label."

"What is it called?"

"*Cut-throat Committed.*"

"I like that. Mine is called *Chopper City.*"

"So what you got going?"

"The same thing—trying to make a hit album."

"I feel you. I like this beat."

"You do, huh?" Daniel said.

"Yea, that motherfucker lives. I got something for it too."

"Let's hear it. Go on in the booth," he said, hitting the blunt.

I walked over to the booth. I hit the blunt and put the headphone on, and went to rapping.

I walked out the booth after I laid the rap down; them niggas was shaking their heads.

"Man, I like that motherfucker there," Daniel said.

"You like that there, huh?"

"Yea, you need to make that your first single."

"Okay, mix it down and shit, and we're going to see what it does."

"What are you going to call it?"

"*I'll Pay For It.*"

"Cool. I'm going to handle it.

I sat a few more hours in there, laying shit down, listening to some more beats. BG and I laid a few rap songs down. Just then my phone rang. "What's up?"

"You coming over?" Dayton said.
"How do you get my number?"
"You coming over?"
"On the way."
"Bye."
"Look, I'm going to fuck with y'all later," I said, dapping them off.

***

I pulled up to some reddish brick apartment. I snorted me a bag of dope. I was going to beat this bitch's pussy up. I stepped out with my gun in hand. In these apartments here in Lincoln Manor, niggas be hustling back here. I walked up to her door and knocked on it. She opened it up wearing nothing but a see-through Teddy. She grabbed my hand, leading me to the back bedroom. She pulled her shirt off. I set my gun on the table, taking my clothes off. She sat on the edge of the bed. I walked over. She grabbed my dick, stroking it and putting it into her mouth, deep-throating it.

She was sucking my dick so good it made my toes curl up, and my eyes rolled in the back of my head with my ass tied up. "Damn! You sucking a good dick," I said, gripping her head, moving it up and down. She pulled it out her mouth, sobbing on my balls and licking my dick head. I was about to come, but she stopped and laid back on the bed spreading her legs. I climbed on top of her, sliding my dick into her wet tight pussy. I put her legs on my shoulders, thrusting in and out of her as she dug her nails into my back.
"Fuck! Yea. Beat this pussy up!" she said, shaking, coming all over my dick.

I flipped her over in a doggy-style position. As I started hitting her from the back, she grabbed the sheets, moaning and screaming out my name as I played with her asshole.

"Oooo. Ooo. Fuck! I'm coming. Don't stop. Please don't stop." She gripped the sheet with her whole body shaking, coming all over my dick, gushing all over the sheets as she came back to back. She got on top of me, riding my dick as she sucked on her titties, biting her bottom lip.

"Yea, ride that dick, bitch," I said, gripping her neck.

"Fuck! This dick is good."

I grabbed her waist, bouncing her up and down hard on my dick as she came back to back. I flipped her to the side, slamming my dick in and out of her.

"Fuck me, fuck me. I'm coming."

"I'm about to go nuts," I said, shaking.

She backed her ass up on me as we came together. I shot my nut in her pussy as she shot all her come on my dick. "Fuck, that was good!" she said, laying her head on my chest as we tried to catch our breath. I grabbed the blunt, firing it up as she got out of bed and went to the bathroom.

A minute later, she walked back into the room, got into the bed, andtook the blunt out my mouth, hitting it.

"Do you know a bitch named Michelle?"

"No, why? You fucking her?"

"No, she got a baby for my man Tre that got killed. I haven't seen her since."

"Why did you ask me?"

"Because she is a stripper."

"No, I don't know all the bitches that strip."

"She got a star on her face."

"I got you. Now let's get back to this fucking. The dick is good and I haven't had one in a long time."

She climbed back on top and began riding my dick again.

Robert Baptiste

Chapter Seven
Soulja

It had been two weeks, and I was fucking Dayton like crazy. It had her looking into the shit with Michelle. I couldn't sleep thinking about my man—Tre. I really miss that nigga. This hustling shit wasn' the same without my dog. As I was hitting a line of dope by my house, my phone rang. I looked at the time; it was 1 in the morning. I looked at my phone, and it was Dayton. *I hope she has something new for me*, I thought.

"What's good?"

"Yea, that bitch works at She She. And drive a red Honda."

"She's there now?"

"Yea."

"Okay. I'm on the way."

"Bye."

I snorted a line, grabbed my gun, and walked out of the house with death in my mind. As I drove to She She, I was thinking to myself, *Should I kill this bitch*? When I pulled into the parking lot, I saw her red Honda. Then she came out wearing some tight blue jeans and red halter top. I wanted to get out and shoot her in the head, but they are having cameras at these strip clubs nowadays. I followed her as she came out of the parking lot. She made a stop, getting her baby. Then she pulled up to this apartment in the east part of New Orleans. I watched as she got out of the car, carrying her baby to the house.

Before she walked in the house, I rushed up on her, putting my gun in her back.

"Please don't kill me, I got a baby!" she cried out.

"Bitch, go inside."

"Please don't kill me."

"Bitch, sit on the couch."

"Okay."

I turned on the light.

"Slim."

"Yea, it's me. Give me a reason why I shouldn't blow your fucking head off."

"Please. Slim. I have a kid."

"You shoulda thought about that shit when you set my nigga up for your fucking uncle."

"I don't have anything to do with that."

"How do I know that?"

"Why would I want my baby daddy killed? I tried to warn him, I swear to you."

I looked over at the little man. I put my gun in my waist and picked him up. He looked just like Tre. I kissed him on the forehead.

"Bitch, you lucky. I know my dog wouldn't have wanted me to kill you, so be glad you got his baby. Now tell me where your uncle will stay."

"Okay, he stays in *The Dog*. He be hanging at the bar."

"Okay, you can tell him I'm going to kill his ass. Here—two thousand grand for the baby."

I walked out, jumped in the truck, pulling off.

Two weeks later, I sat in my truck at this bar where this nigga hang out in South P. I was a man on a mission. I wasn't going to sleep right until I killed this nigga. I spotted him coming out of the bar, walking with a yellow bone. I stepped out of my truck with my .45 in hand. I walked up on him and the chick. I went to shoot him in the face. As he fell to the ground, I shot him some more, emptying the bullets inside of him.

"Bitch ass nigga," I said, spitting on him. People went to running and screaming as I ran back to my truck smashing out. I went to my mother's house, jumped in the shower, letting the blood rinse off me, and at the same time shed some tears for my nigga. I just killed that nigga and I don't know how I feel about it either. I got out the shower and laid across my bed, falling asleep, thinking about my dawg.

Chapter Eight
Soulja

The next day I pulled up to the graveyard. I stepped out with a blunt in my hand. I walked over to his grave. I placed a blunt on his head stone and smoked another one.

"Yea, my nigga, I got that nigga that killed you. I told you I would get him. I let that bitch live because I know she needed to be there to raise your lil' nigga who looked just like you. Don't worry, if I catch my cousin slippin', I'll get his ass too. Well, my nigga, I got to go. I love you always. Oh yea, I got a new pussy. This hoe is bad, nigga. But I'm working on new music, started my own shit. I miss you, my nigga. Wish you was here. It is not the same. Love you. I'm out."

I jumped in my truck, pulling off. As I was turning on Washington, by the projects, a police car pulled behind me and put its lights on.

"Fuck! I don't need these dick-sucking rats fucking with me right now," I said, putting the blunt out and tucking my gun under the seat. I didn't stop until I made it into the project. These motherfucker be on some bullshit sometimes.

I stopped in the driveway with everybody coming out their house, looking. I stopped my truck and got out with my hands up. They stepped out, pointing their gun.

"Don't move, motherfucker."

"Fuck you, bitches."

One came up on me as the other held his gun on me. "What the fuck you want?"

"Your ass under arrest for murder."

Len came out running up to the police. "Na. Na. What the fuck he do?"

"Mama, step back," I said to Len. "Lock my truck and call a lawyer."

"Your nigga ass going to need one."

"Fuck you, bitch!" Len spat at the cop who'd told her I'm going to need a lawyer.

They put me in the back of the police car, pulling off.

***

They had me sitting in the interrogation room for three hours, asking me the same bullshit question about this nigga's murder, trying to scare me. But they don't have shit on me.

"Morrison, should I call you Soulja? We got your fingerprints on the gun," the white police officer said.

I just smiled at him.

"You think this shit funny?" the black police officer said. "You looking at murder charges."

"Lawyer," I said.

"You're going to need one. We got a lot of witnesses."

"Lawyer."

"Your ass is looking at life."

"I need to make a phone call. Y'all been having me in here for three hours."

"Fuck you, punk!" the black police officer said.

Just then somebody knocked on the dark-tinted window. And in walked a slim black lady with an all-brown dress on and a black briefcase.

"Y'all charge him if you really have something on him, or we going right now. So, are you really charging him or just messing with his mind?" she said, with a serious look on her face.

"He can go," the chief interrogator said.

"Let's go."

We walked out the station and Len was waiting on me next to my truck.

"Anita Hawk is my name," the woman said.

"Thanks, good looking out."

"Call me if you need anything."

"Well done."

"Bye, Len," she said, getting in her black BMW.

Len walked up to me, kissing me. "Good looking out."

"Yea, we need to raise my aunt, she is good."

"She is, huh?"

"Yea."

"Let's bounce."

We sat at her house in the kitchen, counting money and bagging up dope.

"How much money did we get?"

"Two hundred and fifty thousand dollars."

"Okay, put it in the bag."

I finished helping her bag the ounces of foil bags up. I gave her $5000. That was her cut. Rell, Craig get their own money when they cop ounces from me.

"I'm about to dipp. I gotta run over and put this money up."

"Okay. Bye."

I pulled up to Kim's apartment. I stepped out, walking inside. She wasn't there. She must be at work. I stuffed the bag of money in the safe and left it back out. I had a couple moves I needed to make.

Soulja

Later on that night, I pulled up on the parkway. They had a bunch of niggas hanging out hustling on the block. I stepped out my truck and dapped all them niggas off.

"What's up, Slim?" Big Willie said.

"Shit coolin'. What's good?"

Big Willie was black as midnight and favored Rick Ross. "Nigga, I'm trying to get a couple ounces of that dope. Nigga said you got that fire boy."

"I got you to hit me up."

"I'm going to fuck with you."

"Oh yea, I'm starting my own label, Cut-throat Committed."

"You know I'm going to fuck with that."

"Later," I said, dapping him off.

I walked into Mike's house, going upstairs where I heard some beats coming from. When I walked into the room, he was on the beat machine.

"This beat is fire. You just came up with that?"

"Yea, something new. You like it?"

"It's on fire. I got something for it."

"Go for it."

I pulled the blunt from behind my ear, lit it and walked into the booth. I rapped a cheese eater.

"I like that."

"Yea, that was for all them rat niggas."

"I feel you. What up with Daniel?"

"We are working."

"The boy fires—"

"Tomorrow."

"Okay, call me and I'll come get y'all."

"Okay. Love you."

"Love you back."

When I walked into the courtway, I saw Peewee was talking to Rell and Craig. *Damn! When this nigga get out*? I thought to myself.

"What's up, nigga? You home, huh?"

"Yea, nigga, and I'm trying to get put down. Hook me up." I got up. "And you're home just in time. I'm starting this label called Cut-throat Committed."

"Nigga, sign me up."

"I got you. Come with me."

We walked into Len's house. I gave him a couple ounces and five grand.

"Good looking out."

"You are part of my crew now."

The rest of the crew came into the apartment.

"Listen to our team now. We going to fuck the streets up with this music and dope, and we are jacking anybody for the paper. This cut-throat shit going to be bigger than *No Limit* and *Cash Money*."

"Do we!" they said,

"Then it's what it is."

We dapped one another other off and walked out the house.

Soulja

I pulled up across the river at *Sole Jewelry Shop*. A lot of niggas in the city come here to buy and make chains and pieces. I grabbed the bag out the truck and walked into the store.

Sole was talking to a fine ass black chick when I walked in. He stopped talking to her and walked over to me.

"What's up, Slim?" he asked.

Sole was an Arab with long black hair to his shoulders. "Nothing, coolin'. I need some shit made."

"Come to the back."

I followed him to the back office, where he kept a lot of real diamonds and gold. We sat at his desk and started talking.

"What you looking to get made?" he asked.

"I've started my own label called Cut-throat Committed."

"Okay, and what you have in mind?"

"I wanted a gold chain with AK-47 on the piece."

"Okay. How many do you want?"

"Five."

"Okay. I'll do it for ten thousand grand apiece."

"Love."

I sat the bag on the table, shook his hand, and walked out. As I pulled off from the store, my phone rang. It was my girl. "Hey, love, what up?" I asked.

"Miss you."

"I miss you too."

"Well, I'm coming to the city to see my mother."

"When?"

"Soon as possible."

"A'ight. Love you."

"Love you too."

"Yea, I know. I just went and got some cut-throat pieces made."

"You serious, huh?"

"You better know it."

"Okay. Later, my love."

"Later, babe."

Moments Later—

"You're one helluva beat maker, Mike."

"That's what's up."

"I'ma send you twenty-five grand for some beats."
"I got you. Okay, listen to this one."
I sat back smoking on a blunt, listening to the beats.
"I heard your known single. *I'll Pay For It.*"
"Yea, got to get it mixed down."
"Yea, that's nice for your first single."
"Yea, Daniel told me to put it out."
"That nigga good."
"I like this beat."
"Yea, drop something to it."
I grabbed the pen and pad and went to write.
"I walked in the booth, laying some rap."
"I like that, nigga," Mike said.
"For sure."
"I'm going to have some more beats later."
"Okay, I'm about to bounce," I said, dapping him off.

Chapter Nine
Soulja

I sat on the porch, hustling bags of dope. I was making money hand over feet. I just bought stacks up to Len's house a few minutes ago. I had the circle bumping with the dope. I had niggas score quarters and ounces from all over. Even niggas in the project was getting dope from me. This shit was going just how I planned it. Just then my phone rang. It was Big Willie off the parkway.

"What's good?" I asked.
"I need to have a brick of dope."
"Okay. I'm on my way in thirty minutes."
"Later."

I went upstairs to Len's apartment.
"Go get me a half brick from the back."
"Alright."

I wasn't tripping on serving the half because it came off the one brick. I was going to charge him thirty grand for it. So, I made my money anyway.

"Here."

She gave me a plastic bag. I stuffed the bricks in the brown bag and walked out the house. I pulled up on the parkway thirty minutes later. Big Willie got in the truck with a brown bag full of money.

"What's good, Slim?"
"Here is the half brick."
"This thirty grand in the bag."
"Okay, good looking."
"I hear that dope fire."
"The best in the city right now."
"Later."

I ran the money machine at Len's apartment. It was thirty grand like Big Willie said.

"How much money you got over here?"
"About a hundred thousand dollars."
"Okay give, me eighty thousand and take your cut."

"Okay."

I snorted me a couple line of dope as I finished counting and bagging of dope.

"We got a half brick left over here."

"Okay. Cool. I'm about to take a dip."

"Want you to stay the night. I need some dick in my life."

"I got to go handle something. I'll catch up with you later."

"Bye then, nigga," she said, walking off, going to the back.

I jumped in the truck. As I rode home, I thought about Len. She is cool. But she is getting played out. My girl's pussy and head is better than Len's, but I'm going to play the bitch for what it's worth. Then after it's over in the streets, me and the bitch is over. I'm tired of her ass. Just then my phone rang. It was my girl.

"Hey, love, what's good?"

"You're coming home tonight?"

"On my way."

"Okay. I'll be waiting."

When I walked through the door, Kim was waiting on me with a see-through teddy with nothing underneath it. The lights were off; nothing but candlelight.

"Follow me," she said, taking my hand.

As soon as we hit the bedroom door, she took off her-Teddy, got in the bed, spreading her legs. I took off my clothes and went down on her, eating her pussy out. She grabbed my head as she started to shake.

"Yes, Daddy, eat this pussy!" she said, with her legs shaking. I pushed both her legs up, as I licked and sucked on her asshole, making her come even harder.

"Fuck, I love you."

I slid my hard dick into her soaking wet pussy as she pulled me to her, digging her nail into my back.

"I love you, Slim."

"I love you back.

I thrust in and out of her as she came back to back. She climbed on top of me, riding my dick in a reverse cowgirl position as I bounced her up and down on my dick.

"I-I-I'm coming."

I flipped her over in a doggy-style position, letting her have it as I finger-fucked her asshole.

"Fuck! I'm coming again," she said, with her whole body shaking.

"I'm about to go nuts," I said, shaking.

She backed up on me as I shot my hot nut in her pussy as she came all over my dick.

She laid her head on my chest as I smoked a cigarette.

"Baby, I love you."

"Love you back."

"I want to go to the show tomorrow."

"Okay, we can do that."

"For real?"

"Yes, love."

"Good. Now let's get back to love making," she said, climbing back on my dick.

The next evening after Kim and I left the show, Sole hit me on the phone. We pulled up to the Sole shop. He had called me and told me the pieces were ready. Kim and I walked to the back of the shop with Sole. He had the pieces laid out. They were all gold with the two AK-47s in the middle of them. I picked it up and put it on. I looked at myself in the mirror and the bitch was glittering.

"You like it?" Sole asked.

"Fucking right. Thanks, my nigga," I said, dapping him off.

"Like them too," Kim said.

"Thanks, love."

I left the shop and dropped Kim off at her apartment. Then I headed uptown. I called all them niggas to Len's project apartment where we sat that the table smoking weed.

"Niggas, I got the chains."

I passed them niggas one each and gave Len one too.

"Now this shit official."

"For sure," them niggas said, dapping me off.

"I love mine, baby, thanks," Len said, kissing me.

"Man, I got a show in the million spot tonight. You nigga going?"

"We're going to be there for sure to rep this cut-throat shit."
"What's up?"
We grabbed our ounces of dope and hit the courtway, serving.

***

Later at night, while I was on the stage performing in the club, I was getting love from the bitches and niggas. As my song came on, I heard a lot of commotion coming from the crowd. Next thing I know, I saw Rell, Craig, and Peewee stomping some nigga out. I jumped off the stage, running over there.

"Bitch ass nigga, this is Cut-throat Committed. You gotta respect us!" they said, as they stomped him. Then his niggas ran over trying to help him. We went to fighting, and next thing you know—Rell up his gun and went to shooting. The whole place erupted in screams, and people were running out the door. We ran to the trucks, grabbing our guns as them niggas did the same. We went to shoot it out. The police came two minutes later. Everybody jumped in their cars and truck, smashing out.

"Man, what y'all was stomping the nigga out for?" I asked.
"That bitch ass nigga was talking shit about the Cut-throat Committed, saying, *Fuck them niggas!*"
"You did that bitch ass nigga right," I said.
"He got served," Peewee said.
"For sure," Craig said.
"I got a song for that."
"What's the title of the rap?" Rell said.
"*Soulja On My Feet.*"
"I like that," Peewee said.
"I'ma drop you niggas off in the project. I have to go to the studio."
"Cool."

I dropped them off in the project. I had to go to the studio in Metairie. When I walked in there, C-Murder was in there recording. I sat down smoking on the blunt, listening to him spit his rap over the beat. A few minutes later, he came out, giving me a huge dap. Me and him go way back to the *No Limit* days, when I was opening for them.

"What's up, nigga?" he asked.

"Coolin'. Trying to get this label off the ground."
"Me too. I got Tru records."
"That's what's up."
"Man, should get on this track with me."
"What is it called?" I asked.
"*Ghetto Ties*."
"Okay."
I walked in the booth and dropped my verse on it.
"Yo, nigga, you like that?" I asked.
"Yea, that shit was fire," he said.
    We sat in there talking about doing some more shit together. I dropped the rap to *Soulja On My Feet* and left at about 1:00 a.m.

Robert Baptiste

Chapter Ten
Soulja

The next evening, I was sitting in the studio watching Daniel and the producer mix down the song. I need to let the street know I was back out here; that a nigga ain't felt off. I need to let motherfuckers know I still run the city. And 2002 was going to be my year.

"What the name of the album going to be?" Daniel asked.

"*Years Later.*"

"I like that."

"Now I need to start getting some more talent on my label."

"Yea, that dope."

"It's all done," the producer said.

"Man, that shit a'ight."

"Yea, they hoes going to eat this shit up."

"You already know."

"I got Wayne to play this motherfucker."

"Yea, you need that radio play."

"It is about this sweet blood and tears."

"Nigga, you better know it," Daniel said, passing me the blunt.

The producer put it on. We just sat back, getting high as my song—*I'll Pay For It*— was coming through the speaker.

"Man, that shit sounds good as a motherfucker" Daniel said.

"I can see those hoes shaking their ass off this," said the producer.

"You better know it," said Daniel.

"I'm out. Got to get some copies made," I said.

"Later, Daniel and the producer said in chorus."

I pulled up to the store, getting 10,000 copies made. Some I was going to give to the DJs in the clubs, and some I was going to put in the record, and some I was going to give away. I first stopped at all the hot clubs in the city, gave them fifty dollars and a CD, asking them to play it in the club for me. Then I stopped by *Peaches Record Shop* and dropped a few off over there. As I was riding around the city, I passed out my CD. My phone rang.

"What's good?" I said.
"Slim, this man Wayne ."
"What's good?"
"Come through in the morning. I got a spot for you."
"That's good looking out."
"Bring a CD."
"I'm on it."
"Later."
Fucking right a nigga getting some air play around this bitch.

Soulja

After hustling all night making sure every store, club, and some bars had my CD, I got up the next morning, stepped out of the shower, drying off. I walked into the room, and grabbed my black boxers and black wife-beater, sliding them on. Then I grabbed some dark blue Girbaurds and a throw-back Saints jersey, putting it on along with a fresh pair of white Soulja Reebok's, with the Saints fitted cap to the back. I walked over to the dresser, snorted me some dope to kill my morning sickness. I put a blunt and hump behind my ears, grabbed my gun, phone and keys, and headed in the kitchen where Kim was munching on an apple.

"I'm about to go," I said, kissing her.
"Be safe. I love you."
"Love you back."
I jumped in the truck, pulling off.

I stopped at the corner store, grabbed me an egg and sausage sandwich and orange juice that I ate on the way to the radio station. I pulled up to the station, sat in my truck and smoked a cigarette. I stepped out the truck with my CD, walked up to the glass door, and walked through them. I met the receptionist at the front desk. "Yes, can I help you?" she said.

"Yea, love, I'm here to see Wayne."
"Okay. He will be out in a minute."
Two seconds later, he came out.
"What's up, Slim?" he said, dapping me off.
"Nothing coolin."
"Follow me."

I walked down the hallway; it was filled with nothing but posters of rappers who have been here before.

We walked in the station. I sat across from him. He put the headphone in view.

"Today we have Soulja Slim in the station. We're going to be asking him questions about his life and the new album. So, Soulja, what it feel like to be free?"

"Man, it feels good. Nothing like it."

"So, what did you go back for?"

"Violation."

"What time did you do it?"

"A year and six months."

"Okay, let's talk about this album."

"Yea, *Years Later*."

"What made you name it that?"

"Well, it's been a long while since my last CD, hence the name: *Years Later*."

"And this new song—*I'll Pay For It*—what made you come up with that?"

"You know this female always asking a brother to pay for the—you know."

"Okay, I feel that."

"So, you're going to stay out this time?"

"You already know."

"Yea, you need to because the streets are missing you."

"Well, you know I'm going to make it do what it does. And hold it down like a big dog support."

"I heard that. Thank you for coming through."

"Thanks for sure."

"No problem."

I dapped him off and walked out. I jumped in the truck, turned on the station, and my song was being played. I pulled off blasting it, smiling, and showing every gold I got. I even went to a couple of clubs that night, watching them hoes shake their asses off my song. I smiled to myself. I knew I had a hit.

Herb

When I pulled up in the hood on the 17th, my crew was hanging out on the corner. I stepped out the truck, dapping all them niggas off.
"What's up with you niggas? I heard this nigga Soulja home."
"So what do you want to do?" Player asked.
"We are about to go through 'Nolia and tear that bitch up."
"Shit, you know about life," Choppers said.
"Yea, that nigga killed the homeboy."
"Yea, my brother."
"Okay, so what the fuck we waiting on?" Player said.
"Let's do this shit."
I went inside, and grabbed the chopper out the closet. I came back out and jumped in the truck, pulling off. When I pulled up in 'Nolia, they had a DJ out there. Bitches and niggas were out there from everywhere. I rode around the 'Nolia looking for this nigga Slim or niggas from his crew. I know they couldn't see me behind the dark, tinted windows. As I rode slow, pulling up around the circle, I spotted that nigga talking to some bitch.
"There he goes," I said.
"Where?" Player asked.
"Right there."
"I see him," Player said.
I parked my truck, leaving it running as we jumped out with the choppers in our hands.

Soulja

It had been a couple months. My song was tearing up the airwaves; it was the hottest song in the city. I was standing in the Magnolia at the DJ spot, watching this fine ass redbone with some high blue shorts on, with all her cheeks hanging out. She was twerking her ass off my single—*I'll Pay For It*—when my O.G Vamp walked up to me, dapping me off. Vamp was five foot nine, with a bald head. He was getting plenty money, and liked fucking them young bitches, and he had swagg like a young nigga. He was clad in a white Polo shirt, red Polo shorts; red, white, and blue Polo shoes with a hat to match.

"What's up, Slim?" he said, dapping me off.
"Nothing coolin. Just checking off these bitches shaking their asses."
"I feel you. You know how I roll."
"Yea, I'm about to go holla at this redbone."
"Okay, nigga, handle your business."

I walked over to her and slapped her on the ass. She turned around, smiling at me.
"What's up, Slim?"
"A nigga trying to fuck that tonight. Where you from?"
"Out of the 12th ward."
"A'ight, what your name is?"
"Rain."
"Let me get your number so I can holla at you."
"Alright. Here is my number," she said, smiling. "And you better all me too."
"I got you, little momma," I said, walking off.

As I was walking back toward Vamp, something told me to look over my shoulders. I turned around and saw two niggas from out the 17th ward jumping out a truck with AK-47 in their hands. They went to open up fire, hitting me. I ducked into the hallway where I had a chopper. Them fucking bullets was hitting so hard. The bullets were knocking chucks out the wall. Vamp jumped behind the dumping, and people went running and screaming.

I grabbed the chopper, hitting back at the niggas. Vamp went to hitting back. Rell, Craig and Peewee went to hitting at them niggas. They tried making it back to their truck. I ran behind them, shooting. One of them niggas fell to the ground as he tried to get away. I stood over him, shooting all in his body and face.

The rest of the crew shot the truck up as it was trying to get out the driveway. As the police was coming into the project, I ran to Len's house, knocking on the door. She pulled it open fast, looked at me breathing hard, as I pushed her out the way, going into the house.

"Boy! What the fucking is going on? Was that you out there shooting?"

"Yea, I killed one of them fuck niggas out the 17th. They tried to catch me slipping."

"Damn! This beef shit won't stop."

"Not when niggas trying to kill me."

I went to look out the window to see where the police were. They had yellow tape around the body. They were going to door to door trying to find out information about what happened. I wasn't worried about nobody telling because we had a code in the project.

"You want to hit this?" Len said.

When I turned around, she had on some pink shorts with her pussy lips showing like a camel toe. My dick got hard as shit. "Yea, let me hit that?" I said, taking it from her, and hitting the blunt.

"Boy, the police deep out there. You might stay in and give me some of that dope dick."

"You ain't saying a word."

I followed her to the back room. She took off her clothes and got in the bed in the doggy style, then I slid my dick into her, grabbed her shoulders, and started fucking the shit out of her.

I got up out of bed later on, leaving Len asleep. I got my gun and a blunt, then walked in the kitchen and grabbed the ounces of foil packs before going outside. That's how shit goes down back here. A nigga gets killed in the day time and niggas back hustling at night. I stood in the dark hallway, smoking on a blunt, waiting on some sell to come, watching for the niggas trying to jack.

"What's up? You got something out of it?" Bee said.

"Yea. What are you trying to get?"

"Three for the fifty."

"Okay, come in the hallway."

I served her as I looked out the hallway, making sure niggas wasn't trying to creep down.

"Thanks, Slim," she said, walking out the hallway. I snorted a line of dope and smoked on my weed, chilling on the porch step. Just then a rap came to my head. I went to my apartment, went inside, grabbed a pad, writing the rap down. As I sat in the kitchen writing raps on the paper, somebody knocked at the door. I grabbed my strap and put it in my hand.

"Who is it?"
"Me, Bee."
I opened the door with my gun pointing. "What's good?"
"I need some more. I need a hundred."
"Come in."
"Here." She gave the hundred.
"Here, the dope. Don't knock on this fucking door no more."
"It's cool."
I sat back down, writing some more raps. I heard a knock at my door.
"Motherfucker ain't listen. Who the fuck is it?"
"Rell."
I opened the door and let him in.
"What's good, nigga? Why you not out there getting this money?"
"Trying to wring these raps."
"Well, it is booming outside."
"Why are you not catching the sales?"
"Shit, I'm out."
"Okay, what are you trying to get?"
"A 4 way. Here is the money."
" Okay. Let's go."
I went to Len's house, grabbed a 4 half of dope, and handed it to him. I looked at the clock, and it was five in the morning. I grabbed two ounces, going outside to catch the rush. They had a line wrapped around the corner waiting on the dope. I made twelve grand in thirty minutes. I had to go get some more dope. This shit was moving. Then Rell and Craig came out pumping. Peewee was on the other side of the project where he stays.

Robert Baptiste

Chapter Eleven
Soulja

I pulled up on the Valence and Magnolia; it was off the chain. This nigga BG had the motherfucker on fire. This was where everybody was hanging in the city on a Friday. I had to push out the project for a minute because the police was coming back there once the sun came up. Plus Sergeant pussy ass was hatching niggas up, pulling a nigga over for nothing. I ain't had time for that bullshit.

I stepped out with a blunt behind my ear and cigarette in my mouth, and a gun in my waist. I walked up to this nigga—BG—dapping him off.

"What's up, nigga?" I said.

"You know me cooling."

"For sure."

Valence and Magnolia was a hustling set in the 13th uptown. They had to set the money side and the murder side. That was across Frete St. Behind the game room. It was a lot of run-down houses where niggas with money was hanging on the line to let the dope fiends and crack heads know that they were interested in getting the work back here. Plus they had a bad bitch around here. BG and Birdman put on the map.

"Man, I heard you killed a nigga the other day."

"You know how I do. I live this shit I rap about."

"Man, we need to do an album together."

"I'm with that."

I lit the Dro, hit it and passed it to him. We leaned against my truck, watching niggas flossing in their whips and hoes shaking their asses. Until some niggas went to shooting at each other. "Man, nigga stay beefing back here."

I grabbed my gun, ducking down, trying to see where it was coming from. I saw a couple of niggas at this red Cadillac truck. I jumped in my shit and dipped. I left there and went to the 'Nolia, grabbed my notepad, and headed to the parkway. I pulled up to Mike's house. I walked in; he was upstairs laying track down as usual.

"What's up, nigga?"

"What's good, Slim?"

"I got a few rap I need a beat for."

"Let me hear it."

I went to spitting *Shit Real* for him as he went to playing on the beat machine.

"That's it."

"I like that," I said about the beat.

"Okay, let me cook up something for a few minutes." I watched as he made the beat. Then I went in the booth, dropping it. "You like that, huh?"

"Yea, nigga, what else you got?" Mike said. I went into the booth and dropped this rap called *Get Your Mind Right*. I stayed there and listened to some more beats. I went into the booth and laid down a rap called *Soulja 4 Life*.

"Yea, nigga, I like them motherfucking raps."

"That's what's up. I'ma come through and drop some money on you for the beats."

"Alright."

Kim

I jumped up from the bed and ran to the bathroom, throwing up in the toilet. This shit happened a couple days ago. At first, I thought it was something I ate. It happened again. I'm a nurse, so I know enough to know I am pregnant. Which I want to be and don't want to be, for real. I always wanted a kid with Slim, but the way that nigga living—I don't know if he's going to be here. I got up, washed my mouth out, and brushed my teeth. I walked back into the room, picked up the phone, and arranged for my doctor's appointment.

"Hello."

"Yes. How can I help you?"

"I need to make a doctor's appointment to see Sarah Water."

"Okay, she can see you at three."

"That's fine. Thank you."

I sat on the edge of the bed, thinking about who I can call to come with me to the doctor.

I picked up the phone, calling Sharon. I had talked to her in a minute. Plus she went through this with Tre. She can give me some answers on what I should do.

"Hello, Stranger," she said,

"What's up? What are you doing?"

"Chilling at the house, why?"

"I need you to come with me to the doctor. The appointment is scheduled for three o'clock."

"Okay. No problem."

"Okay. I'm coming to pick you up."

"Alright."

I walked into the bathroom and got in the shower. I got out a couple of minutes later. I walked into the bedroom and went into the closet. I pulled out a white and yellow sundress. It is too hot in the summer time to wear anything else. I pulled a white thong out of the drawer and slid it on. I didn't feel like wearing a bra. I let the girls breathe. I put on the sundress along with some light blue and white Chanel sandals. I brushed my hair in the mirror, letting it hang to my shoulders. I just got it freshly permed. I grabbed my phone, purse, keys, and headed out the door. I pulled up to Sharon's house in the Eastern part of New Orleans on Lake Forest, blowing the horn. I got out of the truck and walked into her house.

"I thought you said three."

"Yea, I thought we would hang out and catch up a little bit. Nice house, by the way." I looked around at the white marble and big TV.

"Yea, me and Frank moved in a couple months ago. Have a seat. I got to finish getting dressed. Help yourself to whatever."

"Already."

I walked over to the big fish tank, looking at all the fish. I sat down on the white leather sofa, watching *BET*. A couple of minutes later, she came downstairs wearing some tight blue jeans, a pink BeBe shirt, and black Gucci boots. Her hair hung down just like mine.

"What do you think," Sharon said.
"Too hot for the boots."
"You're right."
She went back upstairs and came back down ten minutes later wearing a blue and white sundress, with matching Gucci sandals.
"Now you're straight."
We jumped in my truck and pulled off.

***

We walked through the mall window, shopping and buying thongs and bras from *Victoria's Secret*. We took a break, went to the food court, and got something to eat.
We sat down at the table, talking and playing catch up.
"So you and Frank are getting serious, huh?"
"Yea, he's a doctor, no street shit. He gave me this ring."
"I like it."
"Tre loves him. He took him in like his own child."
"That's good."
"What's up with you and Slim? You still messing around with him?"
"Yea, I'm still stupid and in love with his ass."
"I know. I've been there."
"Slim said he saw you at the gas station."
"Yea, that nigga was mad as fuck when he saw me pregnant."
"So what did you have?"
"A lil' girl. I had a premature at five months."
"What! I'm glad she's alright."

***

We sat in the lobby waiting for the doctor to call me.
"So you're going to keep it?"
"I don't know why I brought you here with me."
"Well, you know I've been through this shit with Tre."
"I know. I love Slim but I don't want to bring a baby into this world without a father."
"So what now? You thinking about having an abortion?"

"I don't know. No. Yes. I really don't know. My mind is everywhere."

"I know the feeling. I was the same way, but I said, *fuck it*. I was going to have my son and give him all the love he deserved."

"I feel you."

"Ms. Smith. The doctor will see you."

"Okay."

Sharon and I walked to the back. We followed the nurse to the room. We sat in there for ten minutes, then my doctor walked into the room.

Doctor Water had been my doctor for five years since I had my first miscarriage. She was slim, brown-skinned with long black hair down her back.

"How can I help you today?" she said, looking at my file.

"I think I might be pregnant."

"Okay. Take your clothes off and put them on the ground and lay back on the bed."

She proceeded to check on me.

"Okay, piss in the cup for me. Then I will tell you when all the tests come back."

"Okay, doctor."

Rell

As I was coming out of the house of this bitch named Keya in the ninth ward, I saw some nigga in a truck parked down the streets. I pulled my gun.

"What's up, nigga?"

Then the truck pulled up fast with the window coming down. I went to hitting as they hit me. I ducked into the alleyway, shooting as the truck went to smashing out. I came out of the alley busting at it.

Keya came out of the house.

"Rell, what's up"

"Them bitch ass nigga Blood and his crew tried getting at me."

"You good?"

"Yea. I'm out."

I jumped in my Benz 500, smashing out. I know I was out of bounce. But I didn't care. A nigga wasn't about to stop me from going nowhere in the city. Fuck them niggas. Blood was the nigga I stomped out in the club. Just then my phone rang. I don't know the number, but it was coming from New York.

"What the business is?" I said.
"This Rell?"
"Yea, who is this?"
"Jackie. From Hunt's."

I had to think about it for a minute. I know a lot of nigga in Hunt's when I was locked up.

"Oh yea, Jackie. From New York, from C block."
"Yea, nigga."
"What's good?"
"Nigga, I'm out."
"For real?"
"Yea. Remember what we talked about."
"Yea. I'm good."
"Okay. I'm going to make a trip up there."
"Do that, my nigga. I'll be waiting to see you," Jackie said.
"Later."
"Later."

Damn! A nigga got their own plug now. I gotta make that trip. I'm going to leave tonight.

***

Peewee

I was in this club uptown called the Warehouse. The whole Magnolia was there. They were celebrating Magnolia Shorty's birthday. The bitch was off the chain. Bitches were shaking their asses off of Slim's song. Niggas was cooling, watching bitches shaking their asses. People were taking pictures with different people with Magnolia Shorty. Everything was love. Until these niggas out the Calliope show up. They walked in there wearing all-black with their face full of hair and dreads looking wild. The

'Nolia and Calliope never got along from some way-back-in-the-day shit.
"The Calliope in this bitch," the nigga Randle said.
"Nolia Soulja in this bitch."
"Fuck that Magnolia shit. It's the Calliope."
"Fuck that Calliope shit. It's about that Magnolia."
"Fuck them pussy ass niggas out the Magnolia."
Next thing you know, we were in a gang fight. Everybody was fighting hoes and niggas from both sides. The body guards pushed us outside. Next thing you know, niggas went to pulling out guns, shooting at each other. They went to hit us, and we went shooting at them. When the police rolled up, one of my little niggas out the project was laying there dead.
Fuck! I couldn't stay.
I jumped in my car and smashed it.

***

Craig

I was sitting in the Magnolia in the circle getting money and talking to this fine ass yellowbone from the other side I was trying to fuck for a couple months.
"What's good, CoCo? You going to fuck with a nigga or what?"
"Nigga, I charge for this pussy. It ain't free."
"So what are you talking about?"
"A hundred and fifty dollars."
"That ain't shit."
"Well, let me get it."
"Okay, let's get to it."
"We can get to my girlfriend's house."
"Where at?"
"On willow."
"Okay."
CoCo was thick as fuck with red short hair, hazel eyes, and big ass butt. All she does is, wear shorts that let her ass cheeks

hang out. As we were getting ready to push, a black truck spun the corner; some nigga was hanging out with choppers and went to shooting. I grabbed CoCo, running into the hallway, ducking the AK-47 bullets. I know it was them niggas off 3 and G. I smoked one of their niggas out this club around the 7th ward; nigga talking shit to me over a bitch, then I shot the nigga in the head. Just hopped in the car that day and smashed out. Now, these niggas—Black and Boogy—trying to kill me.

"Fuck them niggas. I'm going to kill them if they don't kill me first."

Chapter Twelve
Kim

I walked into the apartment the next evening. Slim was sitting on the couch ducking load off heroin. He make me so mad when I see him like this on that shit. But I'm not going to lie that I like that dope dick. He fuck me for hours on in. But at the same time, I hate seeing him like this. I guess I can't have it both ways. But I got to stop being selfish and push for him to get off of the heroin because this shit looks like it's going to kill his ass. I need him to be here for our child. That is why I need his ass to get out the streets. The doctor said I'm four weeks pregnant. I hadn't told him yet, but I'm going to, as soon as he gets his shit together. Maybe a kid will help him change his life. I understand that his music is his life and he raps about what he does, but he needs to now start focusing on his family.

I lost my first baby stressing over this nigga in the streets. I'm not about to lose another one. I don't have any kids. I want this with him, but if he don't get his shit together, I'm gone. I sat next to him on the couch, looking at him, shaking my head, rubbing my hands over his chocolate skin that was covered in prison tattoos.

"Slim! Slim! You got to get off that dope."

He came out the duck.

"Your ass don't be saying shit when I'm fucking you for hours."

"You're right, but—"

"But what? I'm enjoying my high."

"I need to tell you something."

"Damn! Kim, you're going to blow a good high."

I thought about this. His attitude was so fucked up when he get on the fucking dope. You can't talk to him unless it's about some pussy.

"Bond called me."

"A'ight. What is he talking about?"

"He says call him."

"A'ight," he said, ducking out."

"Slim!" I said, hitting him on the arm.

"What the the fuck you want, Kim?"

"When are you going to kick this shit and give the street life up?"

"Right now ain't the fucking time. I don't want to talk about this shit."

"Babe, between the dope and the fucking streets this shit is weighing on your body."

"Babe, I got this. I got this shit."

"Slim, you fucking tripping."

"Ain't your fucking ass living good, riding good? And all your fucking bills are fucking paid, so stop fucking sweat me."

"I don't care about all that shit. I want you to get out the fucking streets and off the dope."

"Man, you know what you was signing up for when you fucking with me."

"Yea, I did, now this is becoming too much for me. And I don't want go to a funeral."

"Man, this is my life. This is who I'm. Deal with it. You're free to leave. I'm not holding you chere."

"Don't play with me." I slapped him in the face. "I ain't going nowhere."

"Bitch, you crazy," he said, standing up with his fist balled up.

"What!" I said.

Just then his phone rang. He walked out.

I went into the back bedroom, fell on the bed, crying my heart out.

Soulja

I walked out the apartment mad as a motherfucker. This bitch put her hands on me. She must be crazy or out her fucking mind. The bitch lucky a nigga fuck with her, because I would have done that bitch something dirty for putting her hand on me like that. I jumped in the truck, answering the phone.

"What's up, nigga?" I said.

"Man, I need a half thing."
"I got you. Give me about an hour."
"Cool."
Somebody else was calling me. "It's me," the caller said after I picked up. I could place the voice.
"What's good?"
"I got some beat for you," Daniel said.
"Cool, my nigga, I'm going to be through in a minute. With some bread too."
"Later."
I hit up Bond. I needed him back on my team if I was going to try and get a nationwide distribution deal.
"What's good?"
"How everything is coming?"
"Cool."
"Okay, you got a show in Mississippi tonight."
"Mississippi?"
"Twenty-five thousand dollars."
"Where at?"
"Gulf Port."
"Cool."
"Later."
I pulled up to my mother's house. I went into the bedroom, going into my safety. I grabbed the brick of dope and 30,000 grand. I had $300,000 cash in the safe. After this key of dope is gone, I'm out. I need to focus on this record label to get it off the ground. I want it to be like *No Limit* and *Cash Money*. I need to start getting rappers from all over the city and put them on. But I need to get this million tickets close to it. I really need to end this beef shit with all these niggas too. This nigga Fav—I need to get rid of his ass. He be in them strip club all the time. I'm going to this bitch Dayton to set him up. This young nigga out the eighth ward—I'ma find where he laid his head and fuck over him too. These niggas better recognize they dealing with a vet. I'm not playing with their ass out here.

***

I sat in Len's apartment, breaking down and mixing up keys. I wanted to make three off this one. I was going to break one all the way down, and the other two I was keeping for niggas that I'm serving ounces, quarters, half keys to.

"What's good, Slim?"

"Nigga Willie, I'm on the way in twenty minutes."

"Alright."

"Look, Len, keep bagging up. I'm going to be back."

"Okay," she said, hitting the blunt.

I pulled up on the parkway. Big Willie jumped in the truck. I served him.

I ran to Mike's house.

"What's up, Slim?

Nothing, just dropping a few stacks of this twenty grand for some more beats."

"Cool, my nigga," he said, dapping me off.

"Later."

I pulled up at Daniel's house. I went to his base where he was making beats.

"What's good, Slim?"

"Just came over to drop you some money."

"Good looking."

"This twenty grand."

"I got some beats now, you want to hear them?"

"I got to go making moves. I'm going to fuck with you tomorrow."

"Later."

I made it back to the project, helping Len bag the rest of the dope up.

"You heard them niggas out the Calliope killed Lil' Poo of the other side? Last night at the warehouse."

"What! I know Peewee and them about to ride on that shit. It's about to be a fucking war."

"You already know that shit."

I hit the blunt.

"Fuck! I just did a song with this nigga C-Murder."

"Well, you know that shit go way back from Glen Metz day and Leslie and them."

"Yea, I know the way back with Black Moe."

"Yea, better stay on point."

"You know I'm always on guard."

My phone rang. It was Kim. She had been blowing me up since I left the house. I didn't even bother to hit her back. I don't have time for bullshit. I got niggas trying to kill my ass. I'm trying focus on this fucking label. I got a lot of shit to be focused on than arguing with a dumb bitch about the same thing right now.

I snorted a couple lines of dope and hit my cigarette.

"That shit fire?" Len asked.

"Yea."

She hit a line of dope and hit my cigarette. The next thing you know, I had her bent over the table, fucking her all in her ass.

Robert Baptiste

Chapter Thirteen
Rell

Jackie was waiting for me as I walked out of the airport. He was leaning against a white Lexus truck. "What's up?" Jackie said, dapping me and hugging me.

"Coolin," I said, dapping him off.

Jackie was brown-skinned, bald, and short. He was in his late forties. He was from Columbia. But he was living partly in New Orleans and partly in New York. He was supplying a few niggas in the city. He got busted with a couple keys of heroin. He took a plea in the state so it wouldn't go fed. He took ten years, whereas in the state you do half and get out. We became cool because niggas out the 12th ward trying to take his shit. So, I stepped in and helped him. Told them niggas he was with me and we could do everything niggas want to do.

"Man, thank you for looking out for me."

"Man, it's cool. Them niggas was bitch anyway."

He pulled up to some nice brick apartment in Harlem.

When we walked in, I looked around and it was laid out. Marble everywhere, big screen TV, leather couches, and hard wooden floors.

"Make yourself at home."

I sat down on the couch, watching the shark swim around the tank.

He walked back into the room with a gold brick of heroin. "This shit is pure. Fresh off the boat."

"Yea, what is it hittin' for?"

"For you, I give a whole key for forty-five thousand dollars."

"What's up?"

"Look at those three fingers."

He slid me three plastic gloves.

"That's why I bend them. That three ounces of raw. You take that back with you. Tell how it works out for you. Then you call me. We do business."

"Man, I can't take it."

"You can handle it. Just ease your backdoor with some lube before you lodge the fingers in. I got a variety of lubes that will come in handy for that."

"Okay."

I stood a few more days, partied, fucked a few hoes and hit a couple. I took the bus back to the city with the fingers in my ass like I was in prison. I went back to my house, shitting them out. I washed them off. I sat in the kitchen in my apartment, opening them up. The smell hit me. I know it was the fire. Pure China white. Yea, I'm about to do my own thing and blow up.

Peewee

I sat on the porch in the Magnolia with my little hitters smoking on some weed, getting loaded off dope. Thinking how them nigga out the Calliope fucked over Poo. Thinking how I need to ride down on this bitch ass nigga Randle out the Calliope. It was Randle who killed him. Really don't give a fuck which nigga I catch out the Calliope as long as them bitches pay.

"Peewee, we got to do something about that shit that happen the other nigga at the club to Poo," Dollar said.

"What you want to do?"

The young niggas off my side looked up to me like an OG. So I got to ride with them.

"Shit, whatever. I'm ready to ride right now!" Diesel said.

"Okay, let's ride."

"That's the shit I'm talking about," Dollar said.

They went inside, grabbed their guns, and jumped in my truck.

I got a bitch I be fucking from back there. She's going to tell where the nigga Randle at. I called her.

"Hello," she said.

"Where that nigga Randle at?"

"He is outside working on his car."

"Okay, thanks."

"What the hoe said," Dollar asked.

"The nigga outside. By Rose Tavern working on his car."

"Okay."

We pulled around the back way and jumped out the truck with guns in our hands. He was just where she said he would be. We ran up to him, shooting him in the face and body, leaving him dead under his car. We jumped back in the truck, smashing out. We sat on the porch in Magnolia, smoking some weed.

"Nigga, that's how you fuck over nigga in broad daylight."
"What's up?"
"Fuck them bitch ass niggas."
"For sure."

Soulja

I got on the stage with a few niggas out the project that I put on my label. I brought Craig with me. Shit was cool; the hoes and niggas was loving my music. I don't know if they know my shit like this. They give me major love. I let them niggas on the label perform their songs, so people could get to know them too. After that, we hit up a few clubs, doing walkthrough at different clubs. The bitches were giving me their numbers. A few of them want to go back to the hotel with a nigga. It was major love. Just then, Len called me.

"What's up?"
"You know Peewee and young niggas killed Randle, huh?"
"What!"
"Yea, them niggas been back here shooting it out all night."
"I knew that was going to happen."
"Alright, get looking out."
"Bye."
"What's good?" Craig said.
"Them nigga killed Randle."
"Damn! I know it's about war time."
"I know."

We left out the club with a couple bitches, taking them back to the hotel where we had a big fucking party.

Robert Baptiste

Chapter Fourteen
Sticky

I pulled up in the Calliope project back town by Rose Tavern in my white Cadillac car. That was when my bitch called me and told me that my OG homeboy Randle got killed. She told me it was some niggas out the Magnolia with that Cut-throat Committed shit that killed him. I stepped out of the car, and walked over to the crime scene where they had yellow and red tape. He was still laying under the hood dead with a lot of bullet holes in his face and body. A couple minutes later, the ambulance pulled his body from under the car. You can't even recognize him. I watched as they put him in a body bag. *Damn, it was fucked up how them niggas did him*, I thought to myself.

After the police and shit left, the crew and I sat on the porch in the project across from Rose Tavern talking about the shit that just happened. See, I'm a Porch Boy, Randle was a Cut boy, but when niggas from outside kill a nigga out of the project, all of us get involved.

"Man, we need to do something about that shit. For real, we can't let them niggas get away with this shit," Spook said. Spook was a Cut boy, black as midnight with a mouth full of golds and a head buster.

"You are going to handle shit in time," I said.

"For sure."

Kim

"This nigga must be out his fucking mind," I said, crying, pacing back and forward over Sharon's house floor.

"What happened?"

"This nigga ain't called or came in a week."

"What! Why?"

"Bitch, we had a fight a week ago and I hit him."

"Kim, you 're going too far."

"Fuck him."

"Bitch, you lucky he didn't punch your head off."

"Bitch, I wish he would!"

"Well, he might just be trying to give you space."

"Bitch! I don't need no space. I need a nigga that's going to be here for me and my baby."

"Try calling him."

"Yea, that bitch goes straight to voicemail."

"Okay, just let Slim go. They have a lot of good men out chere."

"Please point one to me."

"You gotta get out and look."

"Oh, yea, then when this motherfucker find out another nigga is taking care of his baby, and trying to kill me and that nigga then what, huh?"

"You're right."

"Come on."

"Where are we going?"

"Just be cool and just be my wingman."

We jumped in my car and smashed out.

I pulled up in the Willow Courtway, smashing on the brakes. "Hold up, Kim. You got me in the fucking projects."

"Bitch, chill, it not like your ass ain't been here before chasing Tre ass."

"Yea, that was back in the day."

"Well, this now."

I stepped-jumped out the truck with her behind me, ran upstairs to his apartment, knocking on the fucking door like the police.

***

As I woke up, I heard a banging sound at the door like the fucking police. I jumped up, looking around. I had dope, coke, and weed everywhere with two Glock .40 on the nightstand. I know it wasn't the police because they would have kicked in my door by now. So it must be some niggas trying to rob me or something. I grabbed the Glock off the nightstand and walked through the kitchen to the door.

Boom! Boom! Boom!

"Open this motherfucking door before I kick in."

I know this is not Kim, I thought to myself, *outside tripping like this early this morning.*

"Open this fucking door, Slim, I know your ass in there."

I opened the door looking at her and Sharon standing there. "You out your fucking mind. Banging on the door like the fucking police."

"Yea, I lost my mind but now I found it. Your punk ass ain't called me in a week. What bitch you got in here you fucking?"

"What! You tripping."

"Sure the fuck is," she said, walking to the back room.

"Man, get your girl."

"I'm just here for support," Sharon said.

I walked to the back watching Kim going through the rooms. "Ain't nobody in here."

"Where the bitch at? Why the fuck you ain't been home?"

"Because your ass has been on some trippy shit lately. Hitting me and shit."

"Well, you ain't got to worry about that no more. You can stay here with the roaches and the rat. It's over."

I watched as Sharon walked out the door.

"Damn! Kim has been on some trippy shit lately," I said to myself.

Kim

We jumped in my car, smashing it out.

"Bitch, you were tripping."

"Fuck that nigga. I'm tired of his shit."

"So what are you going to do now?"

"Raise my fucking child."

"You told him about the baby?"

"No. Fuck him."

"Kim, you still should have told him."

"You think it would have made a difference?"

"I don't know, but I still think you should have told him."

"Like you did Tre."

"Yes."
"And how did that work out?"
"You know what? Bring me home."
"I'm sorry."
"Just bring me home."
I pulled up to her house; she got out without saying a word.
"Sharon, please don't be like that."
I pulled off crying.

Soulja

I sat in Len's house with Craig, bagging dope up and smoking on weed. "Man, Kim came in the fucking project beating on my door, tripping."
"About what?"
"Because a nigga ain't been home in a week."
"Nigga, a week?" Len said.
"I don't stay out there longer than that."
"Well, she might just be getting tired of the shit."
"Well, she know what my life is."
"Yeah, but she doesn't like the streets like me. I'm a hoe, I don't care what you are, but she's a good girl that like thug niggas. She might just be tired."
"Well, she can get the fuck off."
"Ain't Sharon a friend?"
"Yea, what the fuck that got to do with anything?"
"She saw how they shit ended and doesn't want you to be like that."
"I never thought about it like that."
"Well, I'm just telling you."
"This relationship is crazy as a motherfucker."
"That it is."
I grabbed a couple ounces of bags and headed out. I sat on the porch serving dope fiends, me and Craig.
"Man, them niggas off 3 and G spin on me last night, almost killed me."
"What!"
"Yea, killed one of the fuck niggas at the club talking shit."

"Damn! Everybody is beefing."
Just then my phone rang.
"What up, Daniel ?"
"Fall through, let's get some beats popping."
"I'm on the way."
"Later."
"Later."
"Man, I'm about to dip and be cool. Tell Peewee and Rell where I'm at."
"Later."

Robert Baptiste

Chapter Fifteen
Rell

I knocked on Len's door. I need her to help me mix this dope up.
"Who is it?"
"Rell."
She opened the door, letting me in. "You just missed Craig and Slim."
"Yea."
"They outside in the circle hustling."
"Oh, look, I need you to help me mix this dope up."
"Why can't you just get some from Slim?"
"I got myself a collection."
"Oh, really?"
"Yea."
"You told Slim?"
"For what? He is not my daddy."
"He's your boy, right?"
"Yea, Slim says after he gets off that last dope he's out."
"You're right. Okay. What did you get?"
"A couple ounces."
"Okay. That shit smells strong."
"Straight China white."
"I see."
We went to mix it down.
I snorted a line. She snorted a line.
"Damn, that shit is fire."
I left out and went on my side of the project on Frete, the new side. Nobody was over there with dope because the feds just busted Fat and Whop and took them to jail. So I said, fuck it! Dope fiend still running. And shit still booming.
I stood in the courtway, passing out samples. The fiends were coming back.
"This shit fire, Rell, you got some more?" Freddie said.
"What do you want?"
"Give me the three for fifty."
"Here."

The dope fiends were running all night. I could get a break. I made twenty grand fast off them two ounces; that shit was bumping hard than that shit Slim got. I picked up the phone, hitting Jack.

"What's good, my nigga?"
"That shit is fire. I need you to work with me."
"I got you ."
"Give me a week and I'm going to be up there."
"Okay, later."
"It's on."

***

Soulja

I sat in the studio in Metairie with Daniel, listening to beats and writing down raps on a pad. This nigga had some fire beats shit already.

"I like that one. I got something for it." I walked into the booth, hit the weed and put on the headphone. I went to rapping *Soulja 4 Life*. I walked out of the booth afterward.

"You like that?"
"Fucking right. But look, let me holla at you."
"What's good, my nigga?" I said, blowing the weed smoke out.
"You gotta take this shit more seriously."
"Nigga, what you mean?"
"Find more rest and be in the studio sun up to sun down."
"Nigga, I'm serious. I done drop a hundred thousand in this shit."
"Nigga, I feel you."
"This hustling shit is the way I'm paying for all this shit."
"I'm talking beef shit."
"Well, that's going to be there. Now let's get back to this rap shit." I walked into the booth and laid other raps down. I stayed there till about three in the morning, writing and listening.

Chapter Sixteen
Kim

I tossed and turned in the bed, putting a pillow between my legs; nothing worked. I played with myself in the shower, but a bitch pussy been on fire. I don't know if when you get pregnant the pussy feels like it's on over dick drive. You eat all kinds of shit. Shit that doesn't make no sense at all. It has been over a month and I haven't let Slim back in. He called a few times to check how I was doing. I ain't going to lie—a bitch was about to fall weak a couple times. Fuck! I want him to come over, but I still haven't told him about the baby.

Just then my phone rang. It was him. I let it ring a couple of times. I don't want to show him I was depressed for his dick.

"Hello," I said.

"What, love?"

"Nothing, chilling. What's up with you?"

"I'm outside your door. I need to put this money up. I'm outside your door."

I jumped up, trying to fix my hair, and put some clothes on. "Can I come in and put the money in the safe?"

"Yea, just give me a second. I was just getting out of the shower."

"A'ight."

I put on one of his big Saint jerseys, so he could tell I was pregnant. I fixed my hair in the mirror so he couldn't tell I been in this bitch stressing and hoping he comes home. I walked over to the door and opened it. He was standing there with some black Girbaud jeans, black Reeboks, blue and white Polo with a gun in waist, smelling like a pound of weed, with a black bandana wrapped around his head like Tupac, looking thug out like I like him. The nigga was turning me on. My pussy wanted to jump on his dick. I had to control myself.

"Can I come in?"

"Yea, this is still your apartment too."

He walked in, looked around, then went to the back bedroom, with me on his heels. I watched as he put the stacks of money in the safe.

"You need something?" he asked.

"No, I'm fine. You want something to eat? I cooked red beans and fried chicken."

"Yea, make me a plate."

I jumped up like a kid in a candy store.

I went into the kitchen, hurried up, and fix him a plate, hoping he would stay the night. I watched as he ate the food like it was the last thing on earth, and I was wishing it was me he was eating on.

"So you stay the night?"

"No, I got to go back to the studio and finish this album."

"How is it coming?"

"Almost finished."

"I know it's going to be dope."

"You look like you gained some weight on your face. You're pregnant?"

"I am well."

"Okay. Call me if you need anything."

I watched as he walked out the door, wanting to tell the nigga to please stay with me tonight. My pride got in the way. I went to the bedroom, pulled out my jackrabbit, and got busy.

Soulja

I jumped back in the truck and pulled off, thinking to myself how Kim looked good as a motherfucker. I wanted to stay and fuck the shit out of her. It's been a month. I'm not going to lie, I was fucking the shit out of Dayton, but she was nothing like Kim. Kim, my baby, she got my heart. It's something different when I'm with her. I really love her. I'm going to do right by her someday. I had been in the studio for a month straight. I want to get out a lil' bit. I got off the Claiborne Bridge in the 6th ward. It was a Friday. I know this club called *Escape* be jumping. They be having all kinds of pussy pop out there looking to get fucked.

I give them hoes $150 for some ass and head tonight; I wasn't tripping on it.

I drove slowly, looking around for some bitch that was coming out the club. It was like 4:00 in the morning. The club was about to close. As I drove slowly, I thought I saw this nigga Fav at the truck of his car changing his CD in his trunk. I looked closer; it was that nigga. I pulled my car over to the side and left it running. I'm about to end this beef shit with him tonight. I didn't even have to put my bitch Dayton on this nigga. I couldn't believe he was slipping like this. I ran up on the nigga with my Glock .40 in my hand, dumping on him. People went running and screaming. I ran back to my truck, jumped in, and pulled off. It was so dark under the bridge, you can't really see.

One nigga out the fucking way. I got one more to deal with. I had a few more ounces to get off and I'm out. I thought about going and fuck Len, but I haven't fucked her in a month, so I'm going to go fuck Dayton. But she is getting played out too. I really want to go home and fuck my girl.

Rell

I was coming from the club to load my mind off them x pills. When I drove across Louisiana by the projects, I saw Len coming out the gas station. I pulled up to the gas station.

"What are you doing this morning?"

"Shit, I need a pack of cigarettes and I don't feel like driving through the project right there."

"Get in, I'll give you a ride."

She jumped in the car and lit up a cigarette.

"Boy, you look loaded as fuck ."

"I am. I'm on pills and weed."

"You got some more pills?"

"Yea, look in the glove box."

She grabbed yellow pills and popped them.

"I need to roll a little bit. Shit."

"I passed her the weed."

"Fuck! This Dro is good."

"I know."
I pulled up to the driveway. "Later."
"You can come up. You don't have to drive home yet."
"You're right."
We walked into her apartment. I sat down on the couch. "Give me some water," I said.
"Here you go."
We sat on her couch, blowing.
Next thing I know, she went to take off her clothes.
"It's hot in this motherfucker. I'm sweating."
"Me too."
She walked over to the window unit with some green boy shorts on and all her cheeks hanging out with her bra on.
"Don't be looking at my ass." She smiled as she walked past.
"Girl, nobody looking at your ass."
"You know you want this."
"Girl, you can handle this?"
"Whatever, you want to find out?"
"You fucking with Slim."
"Not no more. We ain't fuck in months."
She grabbed my hand and led me to the back room. She dropped her shorts, climbed into the bed, and spread her legs. "Come put this fire out."
I dropped my pants, got in the bed and slid my hard rock eight inches in her pussy and started fucking the shit out of her.
"Yes, Rell, give me that dick."
I put her legs on my shoulder and beast her out.
"Fuck! I'm coming."
She came back to back on my dick.
I flipped her over, hitting from the back as I finger-fucked her.
"Slide it in."
I slid my dick in her ass as she pushed back on me.
"Fuck yea, Rell, give it to me. I been know you want to fuck me."
I thrust in and out of her as she shook, coming back to back.
"Fuck! I'm about to nut," I said, shaking.
"Yea, shoot it all in me."

I grabbed her ass cheeks, pushing my dick deeper into her asshole, shooting all my hot nut in her as she looked back at me, playing with her pussy, coming. I lay on the bed with my dick still hard. She leaned over, sucking it.

"Fuck, Rell! I'm still on fire."

"Okay."

We fucked until the daylight came up.

Robert Baptiste

Chapter Seventeen
Peewee

I was coming across the Broad Bridge by the Calliope project with one of my little hitters in the car. As soon as I dropped down, a hail of bullets rained down on my car. I tried to swerve the car. But my little nigga took two in the head. I took a couple shots in the arms and legs. I made it to the gas station on broad where a police officer's car was parked at. He came over to help me call an ambulance.

"It's going to be alright."

A couple minutes later, they were putting me in the back of the ambulance and rushed me to Charity Hospital. They rushed me into the hospital taking off my clothes and checking the gunshot wounds. Then a couple minutes later, I passed out. I woke up a couple hours later with bandages and an IV in my arm. The nurse walked in the door, checking my IV.

"You lucky. It could have been worse. Your friend didn't make it." *Damn, Black!* I thought to myself. Just then a few hoes I know walked into the room. Pepper was one of the hoes I was fucking from mid-city. A dark fine thick ass with red and purple hair, she was always clad in designer clothes and had a good head on her shoulders. And the other bitch was from out St. Thomas. She was brown-skinned, thick, and worked around as a stripper. The third amongst the hoes was this bitch named Sue. If nothing else, Sue had some fire pussy.

"What's up, Peewee?" You're alright?" Pepper said.

"I'm cool, baby."

"Why do you call this bitch *baby*?" Sue said.

"Man, don't start this bullshit in these people's hospitals," I said.

"I'm about to whip this bitch ass," Pepper said.

"Who are you calling a bitch?" Sue said, getting in Pepper's face.

The nurse walked into the room. I was glad.

"Y'all ladies must leave before I call security."

I watched as they walked out the room frustratedly.

Soulja

Rell, Craig and I were sitting on the steps in the projects talkng.

"Man, I'm done with the game," I said

"Nigga, stop bullshitting," Craig said.

"Nigga, I'm done. I need to focus on this damn label."

"Nigga, you know in a couple months you going to be back," Rell said.

"Nigga, heard you booming the dope on the New side."

"Yea, find a connection."

"And you was fucking with us on it," I said.

"I wanted to see what the dope was hitting at first."

"Nigga, do your thing."

"Nigga, put me down," Craig said.

"I got you."

Just then, all our phones rang. Then Len came running out the house.

"Your boy Peewee and some other young nigga from back here just got shot up coming across the bridge by the Calliope. He's in the hospital."

"Hello," I said, answering my phone.

"Your boy just got shot up," Kim said.

"I heard. Let me hit you back.

"Is he dead?" I asked Len.

"I don't know .

"A'ight, let's dip and go check on this nigga," I said.

***

We caught the elevator to the 4th floor and walked into the room. He was sitting there watching TV with some bandage on and an IV in his arm.

"What's up, nigga?" I said, dapping him off.

"Nothing, cool."

"What's up, man?" Rell said.

"What's up, Pee?" Craig said.

"Man coolin'. Took a couple bullets in my arms and legs."

"Damn! Somebody else was with you?" I asked.

"Yea, Little Black. He took it to the head, and didn't make it."

"Damn! My nigga, sorry to hear that," I said.

"I'ma ride on them bitch niggas when I get out."

"Well, like I told Craig and co., I'm not selling dope anymore. I'm going to focus on this cut-throat label."

"Nigga, you bullshitting."

"I told that nigga that same thing," Rell said.

"I'm still coming to the project. I'm just not hustling dope no more."

"I hear you."

"You serious, huh ?"

"Yea, trying to get me a major deal. I need to find a new way."

"What I'm supposed to do?" Peewee said.

"I got you if you need something."

"Okay."

"Here, keep the ounces." I placed the ounces underneath his pillow gently.

I stuffed the 250-quarter mill in my bag. "I'm out."

"Later," Peewee said.

"I still be hanging back here. I'm just not going to push dope."

"Nigga, good luck with that shit."

I walked out and jumped in my truck, smashing out.

Kim

I was sitting down on the couch, hoping Slim come through tonight. My pussy was on fire. Plus I was tired of sleeping alone. It's been three months. Either he was in and out or when he came, he slept on the couch because I was too prideful to tell him I was sorry and I miss him. Sharon and I made up. I had to tell her I was sorry. She the one who told me I need to put my pride aside and get my man or let him go.

Just then I heard the keys jingling in the door. I didn't want to look depressed. So I played it off like I was watching TV.

As soon as he came in the door, I wanted to jump all over him. "What's up, Slim?"

"Coolin."

He walked to the bedroom and I got up, walking behind him.

"Baby, you want to take a bath with me?" I was hoping he would say yes.

"Yea, we can. If that's what you want."

I didn't wait. I ran the hot water with bubbles in it. My belly was showing but it wasn't so big. And I kept big clothes on so he couldn't see. I still haven't told him. He walked in taking off his clothes. His big dick wasn't hard. It was calm. But I swear I miss that motherfucker. I took off my clothes.

"You're pregnant."

"Yes."

We sat in the tub talking as he rubbed his hands over my belly.

"You weren't going to tell me you were pregnant?"

"I wasn't."

"Why not?"

"Because I didn't know if you were going to be around to see our kid was born."

"What do you mean?"

"Nigga, you almost got killed a year back. And then you came home wild out."

"Well, that didn't mean I don't want to be here for you and the baby."

"Shit, you shooting at motherfuckers, they shooting at you. I don't know what to think."

"Well, you don't have to worry about that. Because I'm out the game."

"What do you mean?"

"I need to focus on this label."

"When did you make this decision?"

"A couple of days ago."

"What made you have a change of heart?"

"You. Plus shit not the same since you're gone."

I turned my head back to look to see if he was serious and he was.

You serious, huh?"

"Dead serious. I made a couple of hundred of thousand to support us and get this album done."

"So what are you going to do now?"

"Sign some people to the label to finish this album. I got one with BG. I'm working on it."

"So that means no more guns and drugs."

"Wait a minute. I'm going to keep that heat on me. Just because I'm trying to get out don't mean a nigga ain't trying to kill my black ass. And I'm going to always keep a blunt with me."

"Okay, I'll take you coming home and being there for our kids. I love you."

"Love you back. By the way, what are you having?"

"A girl."

"Shit."

"Why do you say that?"

"Because now I got to kill a nigga behind her."

I just burst out laughing.

"Come, baby, I need you to hit this pussy."

"For sure."

Fuck the bedroom. I bent my pregnant ass over in the bath, letting him hit that pussy from the back, putting out the fire as I came back to back instantly on his dick.

Chapter Eighteen
Rell

Three Months Later—

Peewee, Craig, and I sat in Len's house breaking down a key of heroin I got from the plug I had put them down. We were still cutthroat, and Slim would come through letting us know about the new song but then he dipped. I still can't believe this nigga left the streets alone.

"Man, y'all thinking that nigga Slim done?" I asked.

"Well, you got to respect the nigga; he trying to get his label off the ground," Craig said.

"Shit, I got my own problem. I can't worry about Slim!" Peewee said, hitting the blunt.

"Yea, getting out the streets still don't stop that fucking beef," Craig said.

"That on him?" Peewee said.

"For sure. I'm still beefing with them niggas out the nine ward," Rell said.

"Me— I beefing with them niggas off 3 and G," Craig said.

"Shit. I'm still beefing with them nigga out the Calliope," Peewee said. "We got our own shit to worry about." Peewee grabbed the ounces of dope and walked out the house.

"I'm out too," Craig said.

"You need something, Len?"

"No. You're coming back at night?" She tongue-kissed me.

"You already know I'll be back to tap that ass."

"Bye."

I grabbed the half key of dope. Jumped in my car, smashing out. Before I went home, I stopped and served a few niggas. I pulled up on a few niggas in the 12th and 13th wards. And few on Phillip and Clara. I was selling ounces for $2,500. I was moving almost a key a day just in ounces. I was getting 4 keys from Jack every other week.

I walked into the apartment in the eastern part of New Orleans. My bitch Keya was sitting smoking on a blunt. I was still fucking her. We'd been going on a trip back and forth to New York. I threw her the money.

"Count that."

"First, let me suck your dick."

Keya was short, thick, and black as midnight, with purple hair and tattoos over her body. All she want to do is make sex tapes, smoke weed, and ride around with me in my Benz 500. She came over, got on her knees, pulled my dick out, stroking it, then she put it in her mouth, deep-throating it like a porn star. She sucked on my balls and licked on my dick head. She had my ass cheeks tight and my toes curling up with my eyes closed tight.

"Fuck! You suck my dick good."

"You love it, huh?"

"Fuck, right."

She went to sucking my dick hard, slurping on it.

"Fuck! I'm about to come," I said, with my body shaking.

"Come, baby."

I shot it all in her mouth as she swallowed it.

"Tastes good, daddy, you taste so good," she said, smiling, getting off her knees, sitting on the couch and hitting the blunt.

"You're a fuck beast."

"I know."

Soulja

I sat in the studio with a lot of new artistes on my *Cut-throat* label. Niggas was from all over the city. I was trying to put the beef shit behind me. I don't care if you was from out the Calliope, Melp, Magnolia, uptown or downtown; if you could rap, I was putting you on. I was trying to finish up this album so I could put it out at the beginning of August, which was a week away. I needed six songs. I had two done already. I put a couple of my artistes on the song so they can get recognized.

I walked in the booth, put my headphone on, listening to this track Mike did. I brought all his and Daniel's tracks to the studio. I had over twenty-two of them. I went into the booth dropping two raps. First was *Make It Bounce* and *Make It Happen*. I came out and let one of my young rap niggas from out the Magnolia named Deuce go in the booth. I was working on their album too. It was going to be called *Cut-throat*. The first single was going to be: *Let It Rain*. He went in there and rapped a song called *Fucking With This Nigga*.

"What do you think?" he asked me.

"Love it."

I sat back smoking on a blunt as they took turns rapping their song in the booth. Just then the phone rang.

"What's good, Bond?"

"You got a show to do in Key West tonight."

"Okay, what are you hitting for?"

"Ten grand."

"Okay, I'm on it."

"Later."

"Listen, y'all, we're going to go to Key West and put it down."

"For sure," they said.

"I'm out."

I walked out the studio, calling Rell, Craig and Peewee. It was still *Cut-throat*; we were just doing our own thing.

"What's good?" Peewee said.

"I got a show tonight."

"I'm there."

I told the rest of them. They were with it. I went home, got in the shower, grabbed me something to eat, and lay across the bed falling asleep before the show.

Robert Baptiste

Chapter Nineteen
Soulja

When we pulled up to the club called Key West behind Lakeside Mall, it was packed out there. Cars were everywhere in the parking lot on the streets. This motherfucker be packed on a Friday and Saturday. Today was Friday. All the hot bitches was out and all the hot boys was out strutting in their whips.

The club had a line wrapped around the corner full of people waiting to get in the club. I stepped out with the rest of the niggas that was with me. They stepped out of their cars. I had the cut-throat piece on with the Rolex, white Soulja on my feet, fresh blue Girbaurds, and a Saints jersey with the matching fitting cap turned to the back. I had that .40 in my waist in case a nigga gets to tripping with me here. Plus them niggas on my label carry the choppers.

The guards at the door know me. So my little soulja and I had a pass—no pat down.

Bitches and nigga was giving me daps and hugs as we went in the club. A few bitches even rolled in the club with us. That bitch was packed from wall to wall with fine ass bitches and niggas that was flossing. A lot of them niggas in here better be lucky a nigga ain't on no jack shit, because I would have gotten a lot of this fake ass niggas.

I walked over to Rell, Craig, and Peewee. They were already in the club.

"What's up with you niggas?" I said, dapping them off.

"Nothing. Coming to support the *Cut-throat Committed*."

"I feel that. For sure."

"Coming to the stage—Soulja Slim and the *Cut-throat Committed*."

The crew went crazy.

I jumped on the stage, performing a couple of songs off my album—*I'll Pay For It*, and *'Bout Dis Shit*. As I was letting the rest of the Cut-throat niggas rap on the stage, I saw them niggas out the Calliope come in the club. I know shit was about to go down. Because the Magnolia was at war with them niggas.

"Fuck them cut-throat niggas!" Sticky said.

"Nigga, fuck you, nigga!" Peewee said.

"What's up?" Spook said.

Next thing I know, niggas was fighting. I jumped off the stage, getting in the mix, stumping niggas out too. The bodyguard pushed us outside. Next thing you know, niggas went to pulling guns and shooting out in the parking lot. As the police were coming into the parking lot, I looked back and saw Craig shaking on the ground. He had taken two shots to the head.

"Fuck! No! Fuck no!"

I couldn't stay to help him. I had too much going on in my truck. I pulled off fast out the parking lot with my head fucked up, thinking about Craig. I pulled up in the project, slamming on the brake, and jumped out mad as a motherfucker, thinking about Craig. Seconds later, Peewee and Rell pulled up.

"Man, they killed Craig!" I said.

"What!" Rell said.

"Fuck!"

I saw him lying on the ground, shaking but I couldn't help. The police were coming."

"Fuck!" Peewee said.

"Somebody is going to pay!" Rell said.

We jumped in my truck, smashing out. We drove with guns on our laps and choppers in the back seat. We rode around the Calliope looking for anybody to kill. It doesn't matter to us. Somebody was going to pay. We rode around for hours looking for them niggas or anybody out Calliope.

I dropped them niggas off in the project. When I walked through the door, Kim was waiting on me. She was sitting on the couch rubbing her stomach.

"Baby, how the show went?"

"Bad, baby," I said, walking into our bedroom with her on my heels.

"What happened?"

She watched as I put my gun in the closet. Tears started coming down my face. I don't know if I was crying for Tre or Craig.

I just broke down in front of my girl. She walked over, rubbing my back.

"It's going to be alright."

"No, it is not. They killed one of my friends today."

"Where? At the club?"

"Yea, and I couldn't even do anything about it. He was on the ground shaking."

"I'm sorry, Slim. I'm so sorry."

I got in the bed, laying there with my head all fucked up.

Sticky

We sat in the house in the project just thinking about how we kicked one of them fuck niggas.

"Man, you seen how I walked up to that nigga Craig and shot him in the back of the head," Spook said.

"Yea, that's how you do them niggas," I said, hitting the weed.

"Man, fuck that nigga," Black Boy said.

"I feel you. But you know them niggas going to try and get back at us."

"Fuck them. I want to kill some more of them."

"I feel you."

"Me too."

I took a couple more of the weed, dapped them off, and walked out.

"Later."

Robert Baptiste

Chapter Twenty
Soulja

A week later, Peewee, Rell and I were carrying Craig's casket out of the church to the hearse with his family crying in the back of us. We followed the hearse to the projects. Then we pulled the body out as the whole project held second line for him. We passed his casket throughout the whole project. Then we took to the graveyard as we watched them put him in the ground for the last time.

"Man, nigga got to pay!" Peewee said.

"For sure," Rell said.

"Look, we are going to get them. But I gotta go make a couple move. I'm going to catch up with y'all," I said, dapping them off.

"Later," they said.

I walked into the hospital, sitting next to my girl whose belly was big as shit. She had a doctor's appointment. I told her I was going to be there after I came home from the funeral.

"Ms. Smith," the nurse said.

We followed the Asian nurse to the back room. I watched as she took her temperature.

"The doctor will be here shortly."

"Thank you."

"How it feels to be eight months pregnant?"

"Like a balloon." "I love you anyway."

"Thanks for the comment." She kissed me.

"Ms. Smith, you were here for your last check-up?" the white old doctor said.

"Yea."

I watched as she checks out my girl cat. Then she gave another ultrasound.

"The baby is fine."

"Okay, thanks, doctor."

Kim and I went to Burger King to sit and eat.

"Did you find out who killed your friend?"

"Yea, we know."

"Please leave that shit alone. Finish working on your music."

"I'm not going to fuck with it."
"You promise?"
"I told you I would be there for our daughter. I got you."
"Okay. I have to get back to work."
"I'm headed to the studio to finish this album that will be coming out next week."
"Okay. Love you." She kissed me.
"Love you back."

Peewee

Later on that night, I was posted up sitting outside this club across the river in Jefferson Parish called *Caesar* that be jumping on a Saturday. I was talking to this fine ass redbone I just pulled out the club that I was trying to fuck.

"So we fucking or what?" I asked her, signaling her to pass the weed.

"I don't care. I'm rolling with you."

"Okay, we are about to roll."

"Wait, let me go tell me girlfriend."

As she was about to get out of the car, I spotted this nigga Spook coming out of the club. He one of them fuck niggas out the Calliope. I grabbed the gun from under the seat. I stepped out my car fast, running over toward him. With no question asked, I went to dumping on him in front of a group of niggas and hoes. I shot him in the chest and in the head.

"Bitch ass nigga."

I ran back to the car, surprised the chick was still there.

I smashed the gas, firing it to the bridge before the police came. They do not like our police in New Orleans parish. These motherfuckers over here are racist. They catch you on some murder shit, you getting a life sentence.

"Where do you want me to drop you off at?"

"I'm rolling with you."

"A'ight."

I pulled up in the project. She followed me to my apartment. We both was rolling on weed and pills as I fucked the shit out of her.

Chapter Twenty-One
Rell

I pulled up to the bus station waiting for Keya to get off. I had sent her up there to get 4 keys of dope. I spotted her getting off. I walked up to her, hugging and kissing her.

"You good?"

"Yea, daddy, it's all love," she said, grabbing the black bag from under the bus. We jumped in my Lexus truck and pulled off. I sat in the living room at my condo in Slidell, opening the bag and pulling off the silver bricks with the red wrap on them. I smelled the dope through the clothes.

"Here, daddy," she said, passing me the weed.

I took a hit.

"Baby, I'm trying to get fucked. That type of shit tracking drugs and ducking the police got me turned on."

"Come on."

We went to the back room. She got naked, got in the bed, spreading her legs. I climbed in the bed, put her legs on my shoulders, and went to fucking the shit out of her as she dug her nails in my back, coming back to back over my dick. She climbed on top of me and rode my dick in a reverse cowgirl position, her ass bouncing harder as she rode my dick.

"I'm about to go nuts."

"Shoot all in my pussy," she said, grinding on me as I shot all my hot nuts in her.

"Damn! Girl, you are bad."

Soulja

When I walked into the studio, Daniel and the producer were putting the finishing touches on the album.

"Man, this shit going to be dope," said Daniel.

"You're feeling *Years Later*."

"Fucking right."

"Me too. I think it is some of my best work."

"I'm loving it. It might get that distribution deal you looking for."

"It just might."

"It's finished," the producer said, handing it to me. I already had the cover for it. The cover portrays me kneeling down with some raggy blue jeans on, with a blue t-shirt, old Soulja Reeboks, and a cigarette in my hand, while I am wearing my hat turned to the back, with projects bricks behind me serving as the background

"Damn! I did this shit."

"You did, nigga," Daniel dapped me off.

We sat back for a minute, listening to it.

"Man, that bitch sounds good banging."

"For sure."

"I'm out."

"Where are you going?"

"Nigga, I got to go get this shit print up and in-store. I need to move some units."

"I feel you."

"Later." I dapped him and the producer off, walking out.

I pulled up to the print shop. I walked into the store, going up to the counter where this pretty redbone was working. She had on some red tight jeans, a red clingy shirt, and white air maxes, and she was thick as shit with long black hair to her back. *Damn! I'd like to fuck that*, I thought to myself.

"Got a minute?."

"Yes," she said, turning around. "Oh, what's up, Slim?"

"Nothing. Look, I need to get a hundred thousand of this CD printed up.

"Okay. This is your new CD, huh?"

"Yea."

"I'm going to have to check it out."

"What's your name?"

"Tiffany. Let me get your number too."

"I got you." She smiled.

It took over an hour to make the CD. She gave them to me and her number, then she got my number.

"Thanks, love."

I put the CDs in the truck. Then I went around the city, putting them in the record shops and clubs. I even went to Mississippi and a couple spots in Florida. I got Wayne to have my CD promoted on Q93 for me. I had to pay like 25 grand for all this shit.

I also went to different gas stations, putting in there and all the mom's and papa's stores I could find. Now all I had to do was go to a different club, promoting my shit.

Robert Baptiste

Chapter Twenty-Two
Death

I turned on Washington around the Magnolia projects where the Super Sunday was at this time. It be in different spots; sometimes it be uptown or downtown. I came out to see if I can catch this nigga Soulja or some of his crew slipping. I want to kill this fuck nigga and his whole hood. He thought he was going to shoot my block up and I wasn't going to come back. I already killed that nigga nephew. His ass next.

I rode down Washington, looking.

"Man, y'all see them fuck niggas out here?" I asked my crew.

"Na. Na. I don't see this nigga," Dog said.

"Me neither," Wolf said.

This motherfucker was packed with a lot of people, hoes and niggas flossing for them.

"I think I see that nigga."

He post up on his truck.

"Ain't that him with the camouflage shit on?"

"Yea, that's that nigga," I said.

I parked my truck. We got out with choppers in our hands. As we came through, people went to moving out the fucking way.

"We going to overkill this nigga."

Soulja

I was leaning on my truck at the Super Sunday across the streets from the Magnolia. This the shit a nigga be missing while a nigga in prison. Fine bitches walking around half-naked and niggas flossing in their cars, trucks, and bikes. My album was doing well and sold 10,000 copies in the first couple weeks.

I was watching while people passed, showing me love, blasting my shit in their cars and trucks. As I was leaning back on my truck, something didn't seem right to me. I looked to my right. The crowd of people was opening up and people went running and screaming. Then I saw niggas with choppers and guns running my way. I took off running. They went to hit me.

Boom! Boom! Boom!

I ducked in the projects, as the niggas gave chase to me. As I hit the courtway, I saw Rell, Peewee and a few more 6 court circle niggas standing out there. Peewee, Rell and the rest them nigga went to hitting at them niggas as I made in the hallway, breathing hard as shit. I grabbed my strap, and went busting out the hallway. Them niggas started back up, running out the projects.

Damn them niggas almost had my ass, I thought to myself.

"Damn! Nigga, who was that chasing you?" Peewee said.

"Them niggas out the 8 ward. The niggas blocks we hit."

"You need to kill that shit. Get rid of them niggas. That beef has gone on too long," Rell said.

"I told you because you think you got the streets, although the beef still there," Peewee said.

Soulja

A couple nights later, I find out where this nigga Death baby mama lives. I stepped out the truck and walked up to the door, knocking on it. When she opened it with the baby in her hand, I rushed in pointing my gun at her and the baby.

"Please don't hurt us."

"Shut up, bitch. I'll blow your fucking head off."

"Okay, what do you want?"

"Call your baby daddy and tell him to come over here."

"What!"

"Now bitch or I'ma kill your fucking kid."

"Okay."

She picked the phone, shaking and nervous. I hate doing this to this bitch with the baby, because my girl's about to have my child but I'm about to get this beef shit over with. Niggas keep busting at me. Fuck that! I know I told Kim I was going to chill on the streets. But niggas won't let me chill. So it's high time I showed them how dogs get down.

"He is on his way."

"Good bitch. Now sit in a chair."

I tied her up with the phone cord and cut off the light. I heard the keys jingling in the door. I waited until he was in.

"Bitch, why the lights are out?"

I shot the nigga twice in the head.

That was the last night he saw."

"Slim, you won't get away with this."

"Yes, I'll."

I shot her in the head, leaving the baby in there crying. Dumb bitch should have been quiet. I might have let her live. I jumped in my car and smashed out.

Robert Baptiste

Chapter Twenty-Three
Soulja
Two Weeks Later

As I was in the studio with BG, putting our album—*Uptown Soulja*—together, my phone rang. I was hoping it was my girl. She was supposed to be going to the hospital to have the baby. I told Sharon to call me when she was about to go into labor.

"Hello?" I said.

"She is about to go into labor."

"Okay, I'm on the way.

"What's up, my nigga?"

"My girl is about to have the baby."

"Okay, good luck."

I dapped him off and walked out the studio. BG and I had become buddies in the last couple months. Staying in the studio, going out fucking bitches and even getting loaded together. He had become my right hand like Tre. I fucked with him real hard. He was a young nigga that came up in the street just like me.

I ran into the hospital, catching the elevator to the 5th floor and walked into the delivery room. The nurse helped me put my gown on and my mask. I walked over to Kim, kissing her and holding her.

"I'm here."

Just then the doctor walked in.

"Let's have a baby."

She got between my girl's legs and looked under her gown. "Now push this baby out."

My girl took a deep breath, pushing and sweating at the same time.

"You are doing good, push some more. I see the head coming."

She took a deep breath and pushed some.

"Yes, a little more."

Minutes later, I saw my little girl pushed out. The doctor cut the cord. The nurse took it to be cleaned up and weighed.

She wrapped her up in a blanket, walked over to us and handed her to my girl.

"She is 5 pounds 2 ounces, and so pretty," the nurse said. Kim held her tight, kissing her. The baby looked just like her.

"Mom loves you. Mom loves you. You want her?"

I took her in my arms and she felt like a loaf of bread.

"Daddy loves you—Daddy loves you," I said, kissing her.

"What are you going to name her?" the nurse asked.

"Wendy."

"Okay."

Now I really got to straighten my life up. Because I got to be there for my daughter. I can't let her grow up in this cold world alone. With nigga like me that be running through bitches, I'm going to kill one of these niggas if I catch 'em fucking over my daughter. I guess this was God's way of paying me back from all the hoes, bitches, and females I done fuck over in my life.

Just then Kim's parents walked into the room. I kissed her on the head and I was out.

Peewee

I was laying in bed in the projects getting head from the bitch that I met at the club a couple weeks back. The next thing I know—the door came flying open. I pushed her off of me and reached for the strap because I thought niggas was trying to jack me. As I was about to walk out the run, N.O.P.D busted in, pointing their guns at a nigga.

"Put the motherfucking weapon down."

I dropped the gun on the floor.

"Now get your ass on the ground."

"Man, I don't do shit."

"Get the fuck on the ground."

I got on my knees.

They rushed over to me and pushed me to the ground, placing handcuffs on me. They allowed the chick to get dressed. The police walked both of us in the front room, sat us down on the couch, and searched the house. I know I was fucked; I had all kind of drugs and dope in the house.

"Man, where y'all fucking warrant?"

"We don't need a warrant for a murder charge."

"Murder! I ain't killed no fucking body."

I was fucked because the gun I killed that nigga with is in the fucking house. I wonder how them bitches knew it was me.

"Found something."

The police came from the back with a chopper, a half key of heroin, and the .40 Glock I killed the nigga with.

"Take their ass to jail."

"Man. She didn't have shit to do with it."

"Take her ass anyway."

They picked me up, walked me outside, reading me my rights. "You have a right to remain silent. Anything you say can and will be used against you in a court of law. You have a right to an attorney; if you can't afford one, we can afford for you. Do you understand this right?"

"Man, fuck you."

Just then JP pulled up.

Rell

As I was coming into the driveway by Len's house with a half key of raw dope I was trying to get cooked up, I saw the police had it blocked off. *Damn, a nigga got killed back here early this morning*, I thought to myself. I pulled into another driveway, stepped out the vehicle, and looked from the drive to see what was going on. I was spooking hoping it was a Fed raid at Len's house. I walked down the driveway to get a better look. The next thing I saw was the N.O.P.D bringing Peewee out the house. They had him handcuffed. Him and some chick.

"What up?" I asked the police.

"Step back," they said.

Then I saw them come out with drugs and guns.

"Damn!"

They busted him with guns and drugs.

"Peewee, what's good?"

"They got me on some murder shit."

"Murder?"

"Get me a lawyer."

113

"I got you."

I watched them hand him over to JP police. All the cars pulled out of the project. I ran over to Len's apartment. She was standing on the porch watching the whole thing.

I know she knows what is going on. I wonder who this nigga smoke.

"What happened to Peewee?" I asked her.

"Shit, that dumb ass nigga killed Spook out the Calliope two weeks ago in front of all the people at Caesar."

"What!"

"Tripping knowing them motherfucker got camera everywhere over there. And knowing them motherfucker JP doesn't play."

"Man, I told that dumb nigga to chill the fuck out."

"You know that nigga don't listen."

"Fuck!"

"Well, you got the dope. We need to get this money. I got bills. He will be alright."

I pulled my car in front of her house.

I got out with the bag, calling Slim on the phone.

Soulja

I rolled over looking at the clock; it was 8:00 in the morning and somebody was ringing my phone off the hook. I just got in from the studio last night from working on this cutthroat album.

"What good?" I said.

"Man, the police just took Peewee to jail"

"For what?"

"Murder."

"Murder who?"

"The nigga Spook around Caesar a couple nights ago."

"Damn!"

"Well, he said he needs help with a lawyer."

"Okay, I'm going to see what I can do."

"Okay, later."

As I hung up the phone with him, Peewee called.

"Man, what's good? Nigga, what happen?"

"I can't talk over the phone. I need you to go get the money from my house and get me a lawyer."

"Where it is?"

"'Under the dress in the apartment in the project."

"Okay."

"What are they talking about?"

"Nothing yet."

"Okay, my nigga, I'm on it."

Peewee

I was sitting in the interrogation room across the river in Jefferson Parish. My head was fucked up because once they run the Glock, it's going to come out as the murder weapon.

"Fuck!" I hope this nigga Slim and Rell get me a lawyer. Just then two white detectives walked into the room, one wearing a black suit; the other, a brown suit. They both sat at the table with me placing their folder on the table.

"Look, we need to know why you killed the man around the club."

"I didn't kill no one."

"Are you sure about that?"

"Man, I was on the other side of the river in the project fucking that chick I was with this morning.

"The funny thing about that is, they got cameras around there."

He showed me a picture of my car.

"That's your car, right. The gold Lexus."

"Everybody got them."

"You're right."

Then he slid me another picture.

"There you are, getting out of your car with a gun in your hand right.

"That doesn't look like me. It's dark."

"Here is a better one."

He slid me a picture with me clear as day walking over. "You sure that's not you?"

"Lawyer."

Just then a police officer walked in and gave them the papers.

"Oh, by the way, the Glock they find in the house matches the bullets pulled out the guy's body."

"Lawyer."

"You're going to need one."

They walked out. Then police walked in and handcuffed me before bringing me to the holding tank.

Soulja

I ran to the apartment to get dressed. I pulled the moneyout from underneath it. I looked in the bag it had a lot of money wrapped up in rubber bands. I walked out, went to my apartment, and ran the money through the machine. It was 50 stacks. I put it back in the bag and stacked it at my apartment. I walked over to Len's house knocking on the door. She opened it up. I walked into the house. Rell was mixing up dope.

"What's up, nigga?" I said, dapping him off.

"Just getting money."

He don't know I know him and Len been fucking. I don't care. That bitch was the project hoe. I was fucking her no more.

"Len, what your Aunt charge for murder cases."

"Fifty grand."

"Well, you're going to have to get her to help Peewee."

"She's going to want her money upfront."

"I got it."

She picked up the phone, calling her aunt.

"Man, the nigga tripped out," Rell said.

"Yea, he went across the river. He know how them people roll. They white folk don't care nothing about a nigga."

"Man, that nigga was tripping," Rell said.

"Here he goes right here. Hello."

"You handle that?"

Yes, it was fifty."

"Okay."

"Len is about to call her aunt for you."

"A'ight."

"What are they talking about?"

"We'll see what the lawyer is saying when they get there."

"Man, they got the gun and camera with me on it."

"Damn! My nigga."

"Man, these bitches are going to try and give me life. Damn! I fucked up this time."

"You want to talk to Rell?"

"Na, the phone is about to hang up."

"Later. Keep your head up. I'll put money on your books."

"Later."

"Man, what he was talking about?" Rell said.

"Shit ain't looking good for him."

"Damn!"

I dug in my pocket and pulled out some money. "Here, put this on the books."

"Okay."

"I'm going to give you the money to pay for the lawyer."

"A'ight. Slim, nigga, you been acting different."

"How do you figure it out?"

"Nigga, you don't really hang in the project."

"Man, I'm trying to focus on this music. Plus I got a daughter."

"I know. It just feels like you are changing."

"I'm still me. I still hold it down for Magnolia."

"I hear you."

"I'm out. Got to get to the studio."

"Later."

I pulled off thinking about what that nigga Rell asked me. I'm still down with the hood. *Nigga, I rep Magnolia in every rap I do. I m the fucking Magnolia.*

As I pulled off, my phone rang. It was the chick from the print. "What's good, love?"

"Where are you at?"

"Riding around, about to go to the studio."

"Want you come get me? I'm on my lunch break."

"Bet."

I pulled up to the store. She jumped in the truck.

"What's good?"
"Bring me to the daiquiri shop."
"Okay."
We pulled up to the daiquiri shop in Kenner and got daiquiri, then we pulled up on the lakefront.
"I thought you had to go back to work."
"I'm good. Not going back today."
"Cool."
We sat in my truck drinking and smoking Dro. Next thing I know, she was going down on me giving me head. As I was about to nut, the damn phone rang. It was Bond. I couldn't ignore him. I was waiting for him to call all day to see what my album sales did.
"Hold up, love."
I picked up the phone.
"What good?"
"Man, I got some good news."
"What is it?"
"First, your albums sold thirty thousand copies."
"A'ight."
"And second, it's enough that *Kock Records* want to talk to you."
"Who?"
"Kock wants to talk to you. They're an independent company that got major distribution behind them. They sign independent labels."
"When they want to meet."
"They're going to call me and let me know."
"Good looking out."
"Later."
"What up, Slim?" she asked.
I got a push. I'll catch up with you later."
"Damn! Like that."
"No, I just got to handle some business."
I dropped her off at home and headed home. I want to tell Kim first but I want to surprise her.

Chapter Twenty-Four
Soulja

Kim and I pulled up to her favorite restaurant—Sweat, Fire and Ice—on Veterans Highway in New Orleans. I had made a reservation for us. She loved coming here. Plus I haven't taken her out in a while. The valet took the truck as we walked inside. We went to the back where they had a fountain around the table where people ate with fish and light in it. The table was laid with lit candles.

I pulled out her chair, helping her sit down.

"Thank you, baby."

"You welcome, love."

The waiter walked over.

"Can I take y'all order?"

"Give us two steaks with shrimp and potatoes on the side, with red wine."

"Okay. Coming up."

"Damn, baby, you've been so nice to me today. Taking me to get my hair done. Along with my nails and feet. Then you bring me to my favorite restaurant. What's up?"

"Damn, why a nigga always got to do *something*?"

"Because your ass always does. I'm telling you right now I'm not accepting no kids. Me and Wendy going to pack our shit and we out."

"Kids, hell no. I got enough with one."

"Well, I know you still out there fucking them bitches."

"Man, let's enjoy this, please."

"Okay. Baby, I'm sorry."

"Brought you here to celebrate two things."

"What?"

"I got to go to New York."

"For what?"

"I got a record deal."

"Are you serious?"

"Yes."

"Baby, I'm so proud of you. I know you could do it. I always had faith in you. Now, what's the second thing?"

I slid the red box across the table.

"I know this is not what I think it is."

I know I was out still fucking hoes and shit but Kim was my one girl, and I wasn't going to let her go. She held a nigga down through all kinds of bullshit. And never left a nigga side. Why not marry her? Make her happy. She opened the box. Her eyes lit up.

"Damn! This ring is big."

"24k."

It was a big diamond ring wrapped in platinum and gold. It hit me for $150,000.

"Will you marry me?"

"Yes."

She came around the table, sitting on my lap, tongue- kissing me. "I love you, Slim."

"Love you back."

"We going to be working on our second child when we make it home tonight." She smiled.

Soulja

Bond, the lawyer, and I stepped off the plane in New York. I'm glad it wasn't cold this motherfucker. We walked outside; a guy was holding up a sign with my name on it. He was standing next to a black Benz limousine with dark-tinted windows. He opened the door and let us in. It had a small bar inside with every kind of liquor you can name. We made it there in 30 minutes. I stepped out of the limousine looking up at the tall building. A nigga never been out of New Orleans. Everything was big up here. We walked through the door; a black secretary walked up to us.

"Bond and Slim."

"Yea, follow me."

We caught the elevator to the 30th floor and got off on some red carpet shit. They had a lot of platinum plates on the wall from different rap niggas that had their own labels. We followed her into the conference room that had a big round wooden table with a big leather chair going around it.

"Y'all can have a seat. They will be with you shortly to talk to you."

"Okay," Bond said.

I watched as the lady walked out.

"Look, I'm not signing anything but a distribution deal."

"Okay. Let's see what they talking," the lawyer said.

"A'ight. You hear what I said."

Ten minutes later, a white slim woman walked through the door.

"Hey, how y'all doing? I'm Sherry. I'm the VP here. I'm the reason you are here. What's up, Soulja Slim?"

"What's up, love?"

"Bond."

"Hey, how are you? Well, look, let me get to it. We want to sign you to a distribution deal. We see what you done on Hype Records, not on your own."

"We got a deal."

"Okay, what's the split?" the lawyer said.

"We give him a 60/40 split."

"Who getting the 60?" I asked.

"You are, and one video."

"How does the promotion go?"

"You promote, we promote."

"Okay, I like that. Let my lawyer read over the contract."

"Okay, and we give you a million-dollar advance."

"A'ight. Where is it at?"

"I'll be right back. With the check."

"Nigga, it's on," I said.

She walked back and handed me the check.

We shook hands and I signed on the dotted line.

"Welcome to Kock Records."

"Good looking out."

***

The day after we made it back, I put flyers everywhere that I was having a New Year's eve party at the club called the Republica in the C.B.D area. I wanted to celebrate my deal with everybody. I walked into the house. Kim came up to me hugging and kissing me.

"You got your deal, huh?"

"Yea, it's all good."

"What they give you?"

"A million."

"Baby, it's on."

"Yea, I want to get my mother a house."

"What's up? But I thought that goes toward studio time. And videos."

"I got this. Look, we are about to get a house too."

"Okay, not tripping."

"So, tomorrow go look for one."

"We need to put some in the savings."

"You should still have that two hundred and fifty in there."

"I do."

"Okay, we're straight then."

"Come celebrate with me in the shower. My mother got the baby."

We got in the shower, and she dropped to her knees, sucking my dick like never before. I picked her up, pinned her against the wall, inserting my dick in her as she dug her nails into my back and bit down on my shoulders as she came all over my dick. I carried her to the bedroom, lying her on the bed, put her legs on my shoulders, and committed to fucking the shit out of her.

"Yes, daddy, gave it to me. I love you."

I shot all my warm nuts into her soaking wet pussy. We fucked all night until the morning light.

Chapter Twenty-Five
Soulja
New Year 2003

Cut-throat Committed and I pulled up to the Republica. It had a line wrapped around the corner to get into the club. Kim said she didn't want to come. She don't like all this crowd and shit. She said too much happens at night in New Orleans. She kissed me and told me to wrap it up. When we stepped out the truck, the bitches went crazy; we had on our cut-throat pieces. We were camouflaged down. The niggas was giving me daps, and hoes was giving me hugs.

We walked into the club. It was packed from wall to wall. The Republica is really not a club; it's a big warehouse where you throw a big event. Sometimes they would use it as a club on Sunday night. I had the big banner up there with the *Cut-throat Committed* on it. Everybody had on their camouflage representing that *Cut-throat Committed* shit. And I loved it. We got on the stage doing our thing. Shit was all the way live. I was so proud of myself. I did this shit. I finally doing shit my way. After the party, I left with a couple bitches and hit the hotel up. We had all kinds of drugs and liquor. I had a few threesomes that night.

***

I walked into my mother's house and she was in the kitchen cooking. I walked up to her, kissing her on the cheeks.
"Hey, mom."
"Hey, baby. How are you?"
"I came to bring you somewhere."
"Where."
"Just get dressed."
"Boy."
"Come on."
We left and headed to Lake Forest. This is where they have nice houses out here in the Eastern part of New Orleans. I pulled up to the nice house on the block.
"Why do we stop here?"

"This is your house," I said.
"What!"
"Yes, here are the keys."
"Are you serious?"
"Yes."
We got out, walked up to the house and went inside. She looked around.
"This is too much house for me."
"No, it is not."
"How much you pay for it?"
"Don't worry. I signed a record deal."
"For real?"
"Yes, mom. I made it."
"Son, I'm so proud of you. I know you were going to make it."
She hugged me.
"Thanks, mom. I love you too. Here is a check for fifty thousand dollars to get you something for the house."
"Thank you, son."

Rell

I stood outside in the project at the DJ party I was throwing, celebrating my b-day. A nigga was turning 27. I had the project on lock with the dope. I was fronting niggas dope in the city. My plug sent them to me ten times a week. A nigga was balling out of control with a new Benz G-Wagon. I was crushed out in diamond chains and rings. I was even thinking about starting my own label. That nigga Slim did, why not me! I got millions to put behind niggas too. Just then Slim walked in the court way. The whole project gave him daps, and hoes was running up.

"What's up, Rell?" he said, dapping me off.
"Coolin."
"I see you ballin 'now."
"You know how I do."
"You've been shooting Peewee some money."
"Yea."

"Here two hundred."
"Okay, I'm going to give it to him."
"What he was talking about?"
"They can hit him with thirty years."
"Damn! He's going to take it?"
"He's talking about a trial."
"Damn. That fuck up."
"I see you got your deal."
"Yea, nigga, been in the studio."
"I see."
"What does that mean?"
"Nigga, we ain't hanging in a minute. You are good for me."
"What! I'm the same Slim."
"Man, you 're changing."
"My nigga. I'm going to be all Magnolia for the rest of my life. But I got to focus on making move. That's not going to get me since back upstate I'm trying to be out here. I'm trying to last. You feel me?"
"Yea, I feel you."
"I'm going to holla at you."
"Later."

Robert Baptiste

Chapter Twenty-Six
Soulja
Years Later—A Few Months After

I was sitting in the studio listening to a couple tracks that Daniel made for my upcoming album. As I smoked some Dro, Kim kept hitting up my phone. I was getting tired of the bullshit. She keeps posting about the same shit. Me not going home a night, me fucking other bitches. I have been hearing that same shit for like seven years now. A nigga gave her a ring and bought her a fucking house. Plus gave her the kid she wanted. Bitches are never satisfied, I swear. I don't even answer her ass. Because all she want to do is fuss and fight. I don't have time for that shit. I got to put in work on this album in three months. I need to shoot a video and pick out the first single I'm going to go with. Fuck it like this, either you love me or you love me not. That's it. I got the hook to the song I been working on for the last couple days.

"Daniel, rewind the track. I got the hook." I listened to the track, rapping along with it and putting the hook with it.

"Let me hear it."

"*Either you love or you love me not / I'm going by myself / I'm not making no promise I can't keep.*"

"Man, now that fire. You got the whole rap to that?"

"Yea."

"Go, spit it. Let me hear the whole thing."

I went into the booth, hit the dro, put on the headphones and spit the whole rap. "*Either you love me or you love me not / I'll be me / I'm not making no promise I can't keep / Baby, the street made me and I'm going to run them.*"

After I spit the rap, I came out; that nigga dapped and hugged me.

"Nigga, that shit was fire. You need to make that your first single. Niggas and bitches going to feel that shit."

"You like it like that?"

"Hell yea."

"Okay, that's what I'm going to do."

"What are you going to name the album?"
"*Years Later—A Few Months After.*"
"Dope! I love it."
"How much time do they give you to turn in the album?"
"Three months."
"Okay, perhaps this May. Do we need to get to work?"
"For sure."
"What other rap you got ready for?"
"I laid my verse down to *You Not My Dawg*, but I need somebody else on it."

Just then BG walked in the studio.
"What do you need to do?"
"Shit, laying that fire heat down for Slim's new album."
"I know I got a verse there."
"Speaking of one, nigga, go put a verse down on this song, *You Not My Dawg*."

He walked into the booth and hit the dro. He went to spit that fire on the track. That's who I need to make it complete my new album.

He walked out afterward.
"That's it, nigga, right there."
"You like that motherfucker, huh?"
"Love it."
"Man, y'all need to work on the album together."
"We been fucking around a little."
"Y'all nigga to make it happen. I got the beats."
"A'ight, fuck it!" I said.
"What y'all would name the album?" Daniel asked.
"*Uptown Soulja.*"
"Sounds good."
"But look, I came through because I'm about to do a video for it on Atlantic Records."
"Who are you with?"
"Chopper City. My shit. Doing it my way."
"That's what's up, I'm there."
"Tomorrow ."
"Later," I said, dapping him off.

Kim

    Sharon and I sat at City Park with our kids talking. I called her to come out with me because I am on the verge of breaking up with Slim. Ever since this nigga got that fucking deal, his ass ain't been doing right.
    "Girl what's going on with you and Slim now."
    "This motherfucker is a piece of shit."
    "You are still at it with him. You had a good time."
    "The motherfucker proposed to me a couple months back."
    "What!"
    "Yea, this is the ring."
    "Bitch, that's nice. Look, it cost some money."
    "And the nigga bought me a house."
    "Bitch, it sounds to me like the nigga's on his job."
    "Bitch, that nigga ain't on shit. He still staying out late in the studio and fucking hoes and drugging."
    "Okay, what's new? He was doing that when you met him."
    "Bitch, I thought he would change by now. He has a daughter."
    "Bitch! If you thought was going to change Soulja Slim, you tripping."
    "That's why I said the house and the ring shit did matter."
    "It's like this: either way you're going to leave or—"
    "Bitch, I'm in love."
    "Oh, that dope dick got you fucked up. I'm not going to lie, I miss that hour-long fucking, coming back to back some time too, but I love my peace of mind."
    "I know what I want."
    "You want to get that shit with Slim."
    "What do you think? I should?"
    "If you are tired then leave. If not, stay."
    "I'm tired."
    "Not enough to leave that G-Wagon you are riding."
    I dropped her off at home.

I went home thinking about what she said. Maybe I'm still with Slim because of the lifestyle and the millions. I need to get my shit together.

Chapter Twenty-Seven
Soulja

The next day we were on Valence and Magnolia shooting a video for a BG new video. We were riding around in an old white Cadillac going all over the 13th and uptown representing that shit. It was dope.

"And that's a wrap on it," the Director said.

We stayed on Valence and Magnolia coolin' in front the trap house, getting loaded, snorting dope and smoking weed. We sold some dope.

"Nigga, I see you still hustling," a dope fiend said.

"Yea, this is how this shit gets paid for. I'm on my own."

"For sure. The video shit that was dope."

"You like that?"

"Hell yea."

"What's up?"

Just then my phone rang and it brought me out the duck. "What's good, Bond?"

"You got a show to do on Baton Rouge at Southern campus tonight."

"Cool, I'm going to be there."

"Later."

"Nigga, you want to go with me to Baton Rouge to do a concert?"

"Hell yea, I'm down."

When I walked into the house, Kim was cooking some food in the kitchen and Wendy was playing in her pen.

"Slim!"

"What's good?"

"We need to talk."

"I can't right now. I have to get in the shower. I got a concert to do."

I walked to the back room, taking off my clothes with her on my heels.

"That shit I'm talking about."

"This is my job."

"You've got something to do every night."

"Well, how in the fuck you think we paying for this shit?"

"Slim, we got money, it's not about that?"

"Well, what is this shit about?"

"It's late at night and you might not answer the phone when I call you. What if something happens to us? Not spending time. The dope shit and the hoes."

"Kim, this who I'm. I been doing this shit before you met me."

"And I'm getting tired of it."

"I'm done giving you everything. What more do you want from me?"

"How about change? When was the last time you fuck me."

"So what is this about? Me not giving you no dick?"

"No."

I pinned her on the wall, picking her up and ripping her thongs off.

"Stop! Slim! Stop! Slim."

I slid my dick in her soaking wet pussy and bounced her up and down on my dick.

She came back to back.

"I love you," she said, biting on my shoulders.

"I love you back."

I laid her on the bed in a doggy-style position, grabbing her ass cheeks, and thrusting in and out of her.

"Yes, give that dick. I'm coming."

I started fucking her harder and harder.

I was shaking, about to come.

"I'm about to go nuts."

"Come in me."

I shot all my hot nut in her wet pussy as she came all over my dick.

I got up, leaving her to doze off to sleep.

I jumped in the shower. All she wanted was some dick. I got out in a hurry and got dressed. I slapped her on the ass.

"Huh?"

"I'm about to go."

"Okay. Love you."

"Love you back." I kissed her on the lips.

Soulja

When we walked into the gym, it was packed with nothing but bad bitches. They were going crazy. And the music ain't even started yet, plus C-Murder was there which made it even much better. Because we, him and BG had done a lot of songs together. When the music started, they went out of their mind. We ripped the gym up. We took turns rapping songs. Then we rapped a couple of them together. The motherfucker was off the chain. We left there and went to hit a couple up. They shit was live in Baton Rouge.

We took pics with Lil Boosie; shit was all love. After the club, we went back to the hotel with bitches and had a ball. They had weed, coke, dope, pills and drinks. I went into the room with two bitches. BG had two bitches. Murder had two bitches. I sat back on the chair, watching the red bone going at it, both of them eating each other pussy out as I smoked on the blunt, jerking my dick.

"Come, Slim, join us."

I slid on the rubber, climbed in the bed, and slid my dick into one as the other one sucked on her titties. This shit was on fire all night.

Blood

I rode around in the truck with one of my little hitters looking for this nigga Rell. I want to smoke him so bad. I don't forget how him and his nigga stomp me out at that club that night. Plus one of my guys got killed by that nigga. As I rode past the daiquiri shop on Claiborne across the street from the Magnolia, I spotted that nigga car. He was out there stunting for some.

"There that nigga," I said.

"Where?"

"Right there sitting in his car talking to some bitches."

"I see that nigga red Benz."

"Look, get in the back bed with the chopper."

"Okay."

I pulled the truck up to the side of the parking lot. He was too busy talking he didn't even see me. I tapped on the back window for my hitter to do his thing. He raised up blasting. He shot the bitch in the head. The nigga jumped out the car, but not before taking two to four shots in the body and head.

People went running and screaming. I pulled out the parking lot fast as the police went to come in.

"Yes, finally got that nigga. Next time he think twice about fucking with us nine ward niggas."

Chapter Twenty-Eight
Soulja

Later that evening, on our way back to the city, my phone was blowing up. I had a lot of 911 calls from Kim. I hope nothing happened with my daughter. Then Len was hitting me up like crazy. I know it had to be something because I ain't holla at her in months. Then a couple of them young niggas I was fucking with was hitting me up too.

"What, nigga?" BG said.

"Man, I got a lot of 911 calls."

"Damn!"

I dialed Kim's number back as I smashed the gas on the interstate.

"What's good? Is everything a'ight?"

"No."

"What's going on?"

"Where are you at?"

"Is the baby alright?"

"It's not us."

"What is it then?"

"Your friend got shot up last night."

"My friend. Who?"

"Rell."

"Rell!"

"Yea."

"Damn! Okay, I'm coming to the city in a minute."

"Love you."

"Love you."

***

On my way to the project, I picked up the phone calling Len.

"Hello."

"Where are you at?" "In the project."

"You heard about your friend."

"Yea, that's why I'm on the way now."

When I pulled up, Len was sitting on the step smoking a blunt. I walked off to her and sat on the step.

"What the fuck happen?"

"Rell was at the daiquiri shop down the street from the project."

"Okay."

They said them niggas out the nine ward rolled up on him with choppers shooting. A bitch got shot in the head. And Rell got shot all in his body.

"Is he dead?"

"Not sure. The last time I heard he was in critical condition."

"Okay, I'm about to dip and go see him. What's up with Peewee?"

"My aunt said he is going to trial."

"He is still looking at life."

"Yea."

"He needs to take thirty of them thirty. She said that shit off the table at trial time."

"Damn! That fuck up."

"It is what it is. You got thirty dollars?"

"Yea, here you go."

"Good looking, Slim. I still love your dog ass. This still your pussy."

"Yea, until Rell gets well."

"Oh boy, you about that?"

"This is my project. I'm the big dog. Just cos I'm not back here a lot doesn't mean I don't know what's going on."

"You act like you didn't want this pussy."

"I got other shit to do. Later."

Soulja

I had a hella time getting on the floor. The nurse didn't want to let me into the room, because he was still in critical condition. When I walked into the room—Damn, he was looking bad. He was bandaged from head to toe. He had tubes running everywhere all over his body. I hated to see him fucked up like this.

Fuck! Them niggas caught him slipping. I know that nigga was probably stunt in the car fucking with them bitches, not paying attention. I walked over to him.

"I'm going to get them nigga for you, my nigga, don't trip." I walked out the hospital with my head fucked up.

I walked in the house, and Kim met me at the door.

"Hey, baby? You went to see your friend?"

"Yea."

"How is he?"

"In bad shape."

"Baby, I'm sorry to hear that."

"Me too."

"I'm just glad it ain't you."

"It could have been."

"I'm just glad it's not."

Ham

"Man, y'all know where this ass nigga Soulja be hanging?" I said.

"In the Magnolia," Plug said.

"He is hanging in the studio in Metairie," Low said, hitting the
weed.

"Yea, because I don't like how he fucked over Death and his man."

"Me neither," Plug said.

"Well, what's up?"

"Let me call the studio to act like I'm buying time. To see if the plan will work."

"Okay."

"Hello. I wanted to know if y'all have studio time open."

"Soulja Slim got it right now."

"Is he there?"

"Yea, you want me to call him?"

"No, I'm good."

"What they said?

"Nigga there."
"Let's load up."
We jumped in my truck and headed to the studio.
"Man, we're going to shoot that bitch up and everybody in it."
"For sure," Plug said.

Soulja

I laid the verse down in one take. Then I dropped another one titled: *Motha fuck You*. When I came out the booth, the owner told me somebody called for me.
"Who was it?"
"They don't leave a name."
"Okay. Good looking out."
I sat back down fucking with the artistes on my label.
"Look, I'm going to let all y'all rap on this song."
"What is the name of it?" Deuce asked.
"Committed."
"That bitch sounds live," Red said.
"Let's get it. Everybody takes turns rapping."
As we were about to get started, bullets went to hitting the glass window and doors. We ducked down, trying not to get hit by the choppers' bullets that were flying in that motherfucker.
Damn! I wondered who was that trying to get us like that. The motherfucker choppers sound like they don't want to stop. These bitches don't want to stop. Ten minutes later, the police was coming to the studio. I didn't need to have choppers in there myself.
"Look, take them guns out the back door," I told my artistes.
The police came in questioning me for an hour.
"Do you know who that was shooting up the place?"
"No, I don't know shit."
"Well, the owner told us you have some kind of beef."
"Not me. I was listening to music."
"Okay, if we find out you have anything to do with this, Soulja Slim, your ass is going to jail."
"Can I go now?"
"Yea, you're free to go."

The studio owner walked up to me.

"No more business, take your shit somewhere else."

"Fuck you and your studio."

I jumped in my truck, pulling off. As I rode back to the city, I needed to find out who shot the studio up like that. I don't have beef with nobody. I don't think so. I need to make a few phone calls.

Chapter Twenty-Nine
Soulja

"Nigga, what happen at the studio the other night?" Mike asked.
"Man, niggas came through shooting that bitch up."
"I heard."
"Man, I don't know who it was either."
"Man, you got too much shit going on to be beefing."
"I know. You know how this shit goes in New Orleans."
"Man, you been beefing with niggas in the city before this rap shit."
"And you think just because I decide to chill, the street going to chill. Beef never stops."
"I know. What you should do is think about leaving the city."
"Nigga not running me nowhere like I'm some bitch. I'd kill all them motherfucker first."
"Man, you got guns, they got guns."
"Fucking right."
"But it has to end somewhere. I'm just saying."
"We can end this shit. I'm not going anywhere. I'm not going to let a nigga kill me. That's why I got this chopper at your house now."
"Okay, Slim."
"Man, let 's get back to the music."
I walked into the booth and dropped a song. I stayed for a few more hours recording. Then I left. As I was leaving the Dro man house, grabbing me a quarter ounce of Dro, my phone rang. It was the redbone from the print shop. She hit me up a couple days ago trying to get fucked, but I was busy in the studio.
"What's good, love?"
"Shit, trying to see if you have time for a bitch."
"You know I do."
"Well, I need you to come over and beat this pussy up."
"I'm on my way.'
"And bring smoking to smoke."
"Got you."

I pulled up in the project going to cop me a couple bags of dope.

"What's up, Slim?" Redman said.

"I need two bags."

"Here."

I gave him 40 dollars. I jumped back in the truck, snorting the two bags before I left the project. Then I rolled two blunts up. I lit one and smoked it on the way to her house. Fucking this bitch in every hole was all I had on my mind. You know I like turning them red bitch out.

I pulled up to her townhouse in Metairie. I stepped out, putting my cigarette out. I walked up to her door with a cigarette behind one ear and a blunt behind the other and knocked on her door.

"Who is it?"

"Slim."

She opened the door wearing a pink halter top and pink boy short on with no slippers and red polish toes nail. Her hair was pulled back in a ponytail looking like she was ready to get fuck good. She must ain't got no nigga, because she been on my dick ever since the lake.

"What's up, love?" I said.

"Hey, Slim," she said, getting me a hug.

"Nothing coolin'."

"Come on."

I walked into her house; it smelled like peach candles that were lit in her live room. I sat on the couch and fired up the blunt as she came and sat next to me.

"Here," I said, passing her the blunt.

She took it, hit it and started choking.

"Fuck, that shit is good strong."

"Dro, that is."

I took another hit, passing it to her.

She took another hit, choking some more.

"You got a nigga?"

"Hell no. I got time for that shit. I want to fuck and see who wants to see. I don't need a nigga all over me."

"I feel you."

"You probably got plenty bitches."

"Is that true?"

"Most you niggas do. I ain't tripping as long you drop me off some dick from time to time. I'm good," she said, rubbing my dick through my pants. She unzipped my pants, pulled my hard dick out and stroked it. Then she went down, sucking the shit out of it. I laid back, smoking on the Dro. I had her on all fours in a doggy-style position, pulling her hair, slapping her on the ass, and thrusting in and out of her as she grabbed the sheet, looking back at me, and biting her lips.

"Fuck! Slim, you in my stomach."

"Shut up, bitch, and take this dick."

"Fuck! Fuck! I'm coming." She put her head on the pillow with her body shaking, coming all over my dick.

She got on top, riding my dick like a pro. I grabbed her ass cheeks, bouncing her up and down on my dick.

"Fuck! I'm coming again. Fuck! Coming again!"

She came all over me back to back.

I flipped her over and put one leg up as I got in between her, fucking shit out of her pussy.

"Give me that dick, Slim, fuck me."

I slammed in and out of her like she was the last pussy I was going to have. I put her legs on my shoulders, thrusting in and out of her.

"Fuck, I'm about to nut."

"Come shoot that hot nut in me."

I started to shake, shooting nut all in her pussy.

Fuck. That nut felt so good.

I fell on the bed, catching my breath as she placed her head on my chest.

"Shit, that was good."

"You like how I put it down."

"Love it. Round two."

She went down on me, sucking my dick.

Robert Baptiste

Chapter Thirty
Rell

I woke up a couple days later. My body was sore as fuck. I was bandaged up from head to toe, tubes running all through my body. I was trying to remember what happened. Just then the nurse walked into the room. She rushed over to me.

"Okay, don't try to talk. I'm going to go get the doctor."

She came back with an older white woman.

"How are you doing, Mr. Scott?"

"Hurting all over. What happened?"

"You were shot all over your body. Somebody wants you dead, but you were lucky."

I laid back with it all coming back to me: I was sitting in the car talking to this fine ass yellow bone at the daiquiri shop. Next thing I knew, bullets were hitting my car. I crawled out.

"Did the chick make it?"

"No, she died on the scene."

"Damn! I bet them niggas out the nine ward did this."

"You got somebody that has been up here every day to see you."

"You can come see him."

Keya walked in.

"What are you doing here?" I asked.

"I heard about what happened. I been up here every day."

"What's up?"

"How are you feeling?"

"Fucked up. Hurting and sore."

"Well, when you get out we going to get them niggas."

"For sure."

I laid back, falling back to sleep.

Peewee

I was escorted into the cold courtroom by JP Sheriff. I had on a gray suit with gray gator on with my hair fresh cut. The only people that were black in here was my attorney and I. The rest of the motherfuckers was white. I know I wasn't going to have a fair trial over here. These motherfuckers are racist. While I was in, I heard about Rell getting shot up and Slim getting his record deal. And them niggas shooting up the studio where Slim and his people were recording. Len got her aunt to help me with her 30,000 grand. But I know I wasn't going to win because they had tape and weapons. But I wasn't going to take thirty years. Fuck that! These bitches can suck my dick. They going to have to give it to me in trial. I was facing a life sentence. I walked over to where my lawyer was at. They took the cuffs off me. They denied my bail. They said I was a flight risk. They had me with a million-dollar bond I couldn't pay anyway.

Just then I saw the all-white jury—six white older men and six white older women—that sat down looking at me. I saw the look in their eyes. I was through. I wish I had a chance to beat it.

"All rise for Judge Bait, presiding!" the court clerk called out. I watched as this white lady walked in with a black robe on and wearing glasses.

"Y'all can be seated."

She looked at me.

"Prosecution is going to start with you," the Judge said.

"We're going to show the judge without a reasonable doubt that in 2002 Mr. Roger shot and killed Greg Banks in front of the nightclub called Caesar."

"Ms. Flower here, Your Honor, counsel for Mr. Roger. I'm going to prove that it wasn't my client who killed someone on Saturday night in front of the club."

"Okay, begin."

"Here's the tape," the lead counsel for the prosecution said, as the tape began to play.

I watched as the tape played of me getting out my car and running up to Spook, shooting him in the head several times while he was going to the ground.

"There is Mr. Roger shooting Mr. Bank in front of a crowd at the night club. Like a wild man. No question."

"Ms. Flower."

"No question."

"Okay, Jury. It's on you to decide."

"Okay, your honor."

I watched as they went to the back and deliberated for twenty minutes. They came back into the courtroom so fast.

"Jury, what say you?"

"Guilty on a second-degree murder."

"Okay, thank you. Sentences will be a month from now."

The Sheriff grabbed me, placed the handcuff on me, and walked me to the back.

Robert Baptiste

Chapter Thirty-One
Soulja
Summer July 2003

I was posted outside across the street from the Magnolia at Shakespeare Park. I had put together a free concert for everybody in the city to come. Local rappers could showcase their talent. I was going to perform along with Juve, BG and the whole *Cut-throat Committed*. I wrote a song for Juv. I think it would help him on his upcoming album. I was thinking about him when I wrote it.

"What's up, Juve?" I said.

"Nigga Slim, what's good."

"Man, you know me chillin' like a big dog support."

"Man, I see you put this shit together."

"Man, you know I'm going to always hold down for the Magnolia."

"For sure."

"Man, I got some you need to fuck with me on."

"What's that?"

"Man, come by Mike's house later on."

"Okay. You know I'm going to stop through."

"Yea, come fuck with me."

"I got you."

The park was packed with everybody. I just hope a nigga don't come through and fuck it up. I jumped on stage and started it up. I performed a couple of my old and new songs. Juve got up there and did his thing. BG did this. Then my a little homegirl did her Magnolia Shorty. After her and a few more local rap, I sat on the porch in the Magnolia looking at what I put together thinking about what Mike said. A nigga have to fall back some more out the street life. Which I had been doing.

Rell was still at the hospital; Peewee looked at life. I'm the only nigga who survived out our crew. I need to make out for all of us. I might need to fall back from the dope. Cool. But leaving the city and stop carrying guns—that was not going to happen. I need both of them. I took out a foil pack, snorting a line, and hit the weed. "I'll stop, but it won't be today," I said, ducking out.

Soulja

I walked into the hospital room, going to see Rell. Len called me and told me he was doing well.

"What's up, nigga?" I see you got the bandages off.

"What's up, nigga?" He dapped me off. Yea, but a nigga still hurting, plus a nigga legs are messed up. That chopper knotted a nice piece of meat out my shit."

"Damn!" I said, when he showed me.

"Yea, fuck me up. A nigga going to have to learn to walk again."

"It's cool. I'll be here to help you."

"That's what's up."

"Nigga song doing good on the chart."

"Yea, I heard the *Love Or Love Me Not*."

"Yea, I'm going to leave here and shoot the video for it."

"That's what's up."

"Nigga, you really fucking with that music shit this time, huh?"

"Yea, I got to put a few more songs on the album and it's done. Then I'm going to finish the *Cut-throat Committed* album. Then me and BG working on something."

"Nigga, you working, huh?"

"Yea, trying to get it."

"Well, don't let me hold you up."

"I'm out," I said, dapping him off.

"Later. See you in the project when I get out."

"A'ight, Nephew."

I jumped in the truck, pulling off. I pulled up to the house. The video people were there. I was going to shoot a couple scenes here at the house and at this bar. I had my girl playing the chick in the video. I stepped out the truck and went inside to change. I put on some light blue Girbaurds, white Polo, and black Reeboks and my black shoes. I was high as shit. We shot the video in the living room and bedroom. We finished up and went to the bar, and finished shooting the rest of the video. It was dope.

Chapter Thirty-Two
Soulja

I was riding around in my truck looking for some bitches to fuck. But none of my hoes answered their phone. I don't feel like going home tonight. Club 360 rolling tonight. It was a Sunday night. They are having bad college bitches in the club. Along with bad bitches from all over. I know a nigga can pull something out there and fuck tonight. My name alone will get me some pussy. I stepped off the elevator. They had a line down the hallway. The reason they call this bitch 360 was that the whole club turn around. I know the nigga that works the door. I know I was going to have to pay $250 extra to get in with this *Saints* throwback jersey on and tennis shoes.

"What's up, Slim?"

"What up, Nephew?"

"Man, you know *two hundred and fifty* with that on."

"Yea, here you go, Warren."

When I walked in the bitch, it was packed on a Sunday night with fine ass bitches everywhere. Young and old bad bitches wearing tight dresses and tight jeans with their hair, toes and nails fixed. I know I was going to pull me something out this bitch tonight, might be two bitches.

These bitches were in here rolling off them x pills. As I walked around the club, the DJ shouted at me.

"Soulja Slim in the building."

Then we went to play *I'll Pay For It.*

The crowd went crazy, bitches shaking their asses and singing my song. Then he put on *Love Me Or Love Me Not*. The hoes really went crazy, singing every word. I walked up to the bar. The club had two bars and a big dance floor with a big DJ booth.

There was a dress code. You had to be dressed up to the nines or pay $250 to wear a jersey and tennis.

"What's up, Slim? What you want?"

"Jack and a Hennessy?"

"Cool."

As I was sipping on my drink, scooping out which bitches I was trying to take it home, this redbone walked up to me. She was thick with some big dick-sucking lips that had red lipstick on them. Her hair had gold and black weave hanging down her back. She had on a red catsuit that had the pussy print stuck out. You could tell this bitch ain't had no draw on. Asses were big around and jiggled everywhere. Plus she had some nice titties on her.

"What's up, Slim?" she said, chewing on some gums.

"What's up with you, love?"

"I like your song, *Love Me Or Love Me Not*. It's hot."

"Yea, you feeling it, huh?"

"Yea, I'm feeling you too. I was worrying if we could get out here and go fuck somewhere."

"Shit, bitch, we can leave now."

"Okay, let's roll."

As we were walking toward the door, this nigga Kelly out the East grabbed the bitch's arm and pulled her back to him.

Kelly was a big-time drug dealer out the Eastern part of New Orleans. Plus the nigga was a rat for the feds. That is why he never got busted. I was to get him. But never could catch up with the nigga. Plus I had to be careful trying to get him where my ass would not end up being in the feds. He was six feet tall, mouth full of golds and diamonds, and draped out with diamond chains, rings, earrings, with a big platinum watch on his arm. He was wearing black Gucci slacks, a white Gucci button-down shirt, and black Gucci loafers. His hair was cut low in a fade. He was high yellow, and favored the basketball player Keya Martin.

"Bitch, where are you going?" he said.

"Nigga, I don't fuck with you no more." She pulled away from him.

"Bitch, you are always going to belong to me. Bitch, I made you!" he said, getting in the bitch's face.

"Nigga, you better get the fuck out my face."

"What! This bitch ass nigga's supposed to help you or something? I don't give a fuck about this nigga rep. I got my own fucking rep!" he said, booting up at me. I was cool with everything. I wasn't going to say shit. That was between Niece dog ass and that nigga. I wasn't trying to save no bitch out here. I know bitches play all kinds of games in the city. But when the bitch ass nigga went to talking crazy to me like I was a hoe or something, I had to handle my fucking business. The next thing I know, I grabbed the Heineken bottle off the table and went upside the nigga head, and went to stomping him out as he fell to the floor.

"Who's the bitch ass nigga now?" I said, kicking the nigga all in his face. His boys and the bouncers came running over there, trying to grab me. I pushed them off me and headed for the door with the hoe on my heels.

"Nigga, this shit ain't over," he said, getting up off the floor, holding his head with blood coming from it.

"Nigga, you know where to find me. In the Magnolia. I'll be waiting!" I said, walking out the door.

We jumped in the truck, smashing out.

I laid back in the hotel bed, watching as this freak bitch deep-throat my dick and licked my balls. I grabbed her head, pushing up and down on my dick as she slopped and choked on it. Then she climbed on top of me in a reverse cowgirl position, slamming her ass down on my dick. I stuck my finger in her asshole as she came all over my dick.

"Fuck! Yea, I'm coming again, Slim!"

I flipped her over, putting both legs on my shoulders, and went to fucking the shit out of her. She dug her nail in my back as I slammed my dick deep into her pussy walls.

"Oh shit, Slim, you in my stomach. Wait a minute."

She got in a doggy-style position. I grabbed her ass cheeks and spread them, slamming my dick deeper in her soaking wet pussy. She put her head on the pillow screaming out my name. I was putting that dope dick on this bitch. I pulled out and slid in her asshole. She slid back on me like it wasn't anything; the bitch's asshole was wet just like her pussy.

I went to fucking her like a dog.

"Oh fuck! Oh, fuck me. I'm coming.

I was shaking.

"I'm about to go nuts."

"Yea, come for me, Slim."

I pulled my dick out shooting nuts all over this bitches back.

"Fuck! Yea, Daddy."

I jumped out of bed and put my clothes on.

"Damn! Slim, that's how you're going to leave a bitch."

"If you want a ride you better be getting your clothes on."

I walked into the bathroom, took a piss, came out, grabbed my gun and keys, and headed out the door with her on my heels.

I never sleep with a dog bitch. The only thing they're good for is bust a nut in their mouth, pussy, and asshole.

Kelly

I rode around the city thing about how this bitches nigga Soulja Slim shines on me in front of all the people in the club. That bitch ass nigga must have forgot who I'm. I run this motherfucker. He thinks because I'm working for the feds I want to get him knocked off. I'm not the kind of nigga to fuck with! I'll send your ass to the feds or get you knocked. Then he shines on me in front of this dog bitch. That's my home. That dog bitch calling me now probably wants to lick my balls and eat my asshole. That bitch knows who takes care of her. This nigga Slim got to go. He shine on me and fucked my hoe, it over for that nigga. He is going to be like 2Pac. Gonna RIP this nigga. I pulled up in the seven on this dark side niggas; they always down for making money and fucking niggas up.

Ward

I was sitting on the steps in the 7th on Frenchman with a .40 on my lap talking to a few of my niggas smoking weed and hustling dope. Then this nigga Kelly pulled up in his green Lexus truck. This nigga was giving the whole hood heroin. I'm talking fire dope. He rolled down the window.

"Ward, come holla at me."

I walked over and got in the nigga car.

"What's up, Kelly?"

He pulled off, passing me the dro.

I hit it."

"Look, I got a key of raw on this nigga Soulja Slim head."

"The rap nigga from uptown?"
"Yea."
"What's good?"
"The nigga shine on me in the club the other night in front of my bitch and a lot of people."
"Word."
"Yea, I need that nigga gone."
"No problem, I got you," I said, dapping the nigga off.
He pulled back up on my set.
I stepped out walked over to the crew and sat on the steps.
"What that nigga Kelly wanted?" Dog said.
"Shit, to get a nigga killed?"
"Who would be like that there?" Pit asked.
"Soulja Slim."
"What he talking?" Dog asked.
"A key of heroin."
"Yea," Pit said.
"That nigga dead?" Dog said.
"You already know."

Chapter Thirty-Three
Soulja Slim

I sat on the porch steps in the Magnolia, smoking on a hump cigarette, talking to this O.G nigga Charles Brown. He was O.G Vamp's cousin. A real pretty boy type that be fucking all the young bitches in the city. High yellow ass nigga that stay clean and shave all the time. The nigga been getting money for years jacking and selling dope. He is going to stay with keys of something, whether it's dope or coke. And stay driving in a clean car. He got the big white BMW that all the bitches jocking in the city.

"What's up, Slim?" he said, smoking on a blunt.

"Nigga, what up with you?"

"You know me trying to catch the morning rush."

"I hear you."

"I heard about that shit in the club last night."

"Yea, sucker ass nigga Kelly out the east tripping on that dog bitch Niece out of St. Thomas."

"Shit, everybody done fuck that bitch in the city. I hit that bitch in her asshole."

"I did too."

We laughed.

"Man, that bitch been hoeing out since she was young. She get it from her mother."

"Yea."

"Her mother was tricking back in the day with all the baller niggas."

"I'm not tripping over that bitch ."

"Yea, you got them tender dick nigga that will kill you over a hoe."

"Ain't that cool."

"Yea, them hoes don't even want them nigga. Because they know them nigga be fake."

"For sure."

"But you need to watch that nigga. He be putting money over niggas."

"Yea, fuck that rat nigga."

"I'm just telling you."
"Yea, he better kill. If not I'm going to fuck over him."
"I heard you, Slim."
"Good looking though."
"No problem."
"I'm about to dip."
"Later, Slim, be cool."
"You already know, Nephew," I said, dapping him off.

Soulja Slim

I went to the studio to put the last touch on my album before I turned it in to the record company. Daniel had a few more tracks for me to rap over. I needed three to four raps to complete the album. I walked into the booth thinking about this bitch ass nigga Kelly and rapped *Cheese Eater*, *Yeah*, *Heat On Me*, *Magnolia*. These were the last songs I needed to complete the album.
"You like them?" I asked.
"Yea, them motherfucker live."
"Good. I should get a gold album out of this motherfucker."
"Most def."
Just then BG walked into the studio.
"What's good with you niggas?"
"Coolin', finishing the last touch on the album."
"What's up? What's up with that shit last night?"
"That straight old bitch ass nigga tripping about dog bitch that the whole city done fuck."
"Man, I don't know what's wrong with these niggas in the city falling in love with these dog ass hoes."
"They want a real nigga to fuck them up. That's all."
"On the real."
"When y'all going to finish the album?"
"We got a few more songs on them."
"Okay, let me know something."
"I'm out," BG said.
"That's cool."
"What's up with the Cut-throat Committed album?"
"It's going to come out right after this one."

"Okay, holla at me. I got the beats."
"You already know, Nephew. I got you."
"Cool."
I stayed in there fucking with Daniel the whole day.
"Man, look, give me a couple days to mix and master the album."
"A'ight."

Robert Baptiste

Chapter Thirty-Four
Soulja Slim
August 2003

I walked into Q93 radio station, smoking a whole pound of dro. I had just come back from New York City, giving the record label the album. They liked it. They told me I need to pick another single off the album. *Love Me Or Love Me* not was going well. Plus after I leave here, I gotta go meet Juve. I got this song I wrote for him.

"What's up, Slim?"

"Coolin'."

I followed him to the back. We went to the station. I had my black shades on. I was high off that dro and dope. It was really too early for me to get up. But I need the radio play and the nigga was fucking with me a long way back since my first album.

"So, Slim, you back again, huh? How does it feel?"

"Man, this is the first time I really stay out to enjoy an album."

"I know, right."

"So I see *Love Me Or Love Me* not going at it on the chart."

"Yea, you know how I do."

"When is the album coming out?"

"Sometime this month."

"Okay, what is going to be the next single?"

"*You're Going To Feel Me*."

"Like that. Whatever you're going on about?"

"Cut-throat Committed and me and BG album—*Uptown Soulja*."

"Look like you're working."

"Yea, putting it down."

"What next?"

"Sign other people. You know, put the city on."

"Feel that."

"I got my album release party at the House of Blue. In two weeks."

"That's what's up. Y'all heard it here first. Album release party."

"Thanks for the love."
"No problem, Slim, you know you're family."

***

Two Weeks Later

I pulled up to the House of Blues. It was packed a line around the corner to get in the place. It was an all-black album release party. My album dropped. I was hoping to get gold. I stepped out; niggas and hoes was giving me daps and hugs. When I stepped into the club, it was packed from wall to wall with bad bitches in black tights and jeans. Niggas were in there to dress in all-black with a bling jewelry stunt for the bitches. The whole Magnolia was in the bitch to represent the hood and show out for me. I had on the black Girbaud's, all-black Polo, with the Soulja Reeboks.

I got on the stage with the *Cut-throat Committed* performing songs from the album and the up-and-coming album. Plus BG got on the stage, performing with me. The club was off the chain.

I sat back in the club, watching the committed doing their thing. As I got a load of coke, dope, and pills, I left the club at about three in the morning. I went to the hotel with a couple of bad bitches. When we got to the hotel, I had a change of heart.

I left them there and went home. I walked into the room Kim was sleeping in. I got in bed with her, wrapped my arms around her, and went to sleep.

"Love you, Slim," she said, "Love you back."

Chapter Thirty-Five
Soulja
Nov

I stepped out the shower, drying off, rushing to get dressed. I looked at the time it was 8:30p.m. I had a show at the lakefront area. But I needed to make a couple stops. I had to pick up a few Cut-throat Committed niggas. I had to get some Dro, and dope.

Kim went to her mother for Thanksgiving with the baby.

We've been doing well. I've been coming at night. We been talking about we are going to rehab to kick this dope habit. But I was going to kick the weed. My album was doing good; it went gold, and sold 700,000. A nigga was seeing a few dollars. I grabbed my black wife-beater and black boxers, sliding them on. Then I slid on my camouflage fit with my black boots. I grabbed two grand and stuck it in my pocket. I grabbed my .40 Glock, along with my keys and phone, and headed for the door. I got in the truck lighting up a blunt before pulling off.

The first stop I made was at my mother's house. I walked in looking for her. She was in the kitchen cooking as usual for Thanksgiving eve.

"What's up, mom? Just stopped by checking on you to tell you I love you and happy thanksgiving."

"Same here. I love you and am proud of you."

"Thanks, I gotta go. I got a show to go to."

"Alright, baby, be safe.

"Alright."

I pulled up to Deuce's house first, blowing the horn. He came out with all his camouflage on, getting in the truck smelling like a pound of weed.

"What up, nigga? You are ready to show out?"

"You already know."

"This shit going to be live."

Then I pulled up to Lil' Red's house. He came out wearing the same thing, jumping in the truck.

"What's up nigga?"

"Coolin, ready to put on for the city."

"For sure."

"I got to go to the studio right fast. The nigga Player over there. Then I got to stop and get some Dro and some dope."

"We cool with that."

Ward

I was waiting for this nigga to come to the studio. I had a nigga to let me know when he was coming. I had dressed in all-black with a hood on my head. I was waiting behind the studio building for at least an hour. Just then, I saw his truck pull up. As he stepped out the truck and walked up to the studio, I stepped out shooting at him. The first one missed but the next two bullets hit him in the chest, causing him to fall to the ground. I ran over to him, shooting him three times in the face. I made sure he was dead. Then I took his Rolex and his chain. I looked up and the rest them niggas was jumping out the truck, running.

"Oh, bitch ass niggas!" I said.

I ran to the car, jumping in and pulling off.

As I hit the interstate, I called Kelly.

"What's up?"

"It's done."

"Good."

"I'm on my way."

When I walked in his house, I saw Kelly waiting for me.

"What's up, my nigga?" he said.

"Here to get the brick."

I picked up the brick and walked out the house.

Kim

As I was in the kitchen at my mother's house, my aunt came running in the kitchen.

"Kim, you need to check out the news."

"What! Why!"

"They talking about Slim."

I ran in the living room, turning up the TV.

At first, I saw yellow and red tape. I thought he killed somebody but when I turned the TV up some more, I was shocked.

"Breaking News. Today Morris Brown, better known as Soulja Slim, was murdered."

"Murder! No, that got to be a joke."

Then they showed his body on the ground.

"Lord! Please! Lord, no."

I fell on the floor on my knees, crying my heart out. My head was messed up. I couldn't think. I just talked to him a couple minutes ago. This shit can't be happening to me. I got a lil' girl to raise.

"Baby, it's going to be alright," my mother said, rubbing my back.

I got up and ran to the bathroom.

What the fuck am I going to do now? I'm pregnant with my second child. I was going to tell him tonight when he got back from the concert.

"Fuck! Shit is fucked up," I said, throwing up again.

Rell

I stood on Canal St., watching as the whole city came out to mourn Soulja Slim, my nigga. I watched as the white horses and white carriage with an open glass with the gold casket in it passed by the crowd and me. I watched as people cried and shed tears. It was a fuck up day in the city. I was in the hospital then. I heard it was Kelly who put the hit on him, and niggas out the seven ward took the hit. Don't trip because I got change on his head to both of them. I followed the horse and carriage to the project.

Then the second line started; as they pulled his casket out the carriage, niggas went to the second line with his casket. Then the music stopped. And somebody put on his music.

It was just like a Biggie Smalls funeral. They cut up for him. It was a beautiful thing that Soulja had so much love. He was the real Magnolia Soulja. R.I.P. MAGNOLIA SLIM.

Kim

After the funeral, a couple days later, I went home and cried for a week straight about him. I packed my stuff. I couldn't be in New Orleans any more. I had made up mind I was out. I was a couple weeks pregnant. I was having a boy. But I wasn't going to raise him in New Orleans. I was going to give him a chance. I jumped on the plane back to the A. My house was still on the market and nobody had bought it. I got back. I took a deep breath and cried a little. But when I land in the Atl., everything will be good.

Peewee

Here I'm on the white bus headed upstate to Angola with a life sentence. I was already fucked up when they gave me a life sentence. But now I'm really fucked up now. Heard about my nigga Soulja Slim getting killed. That shit got my headed all fuck up. A bitch a nigga killed him for a penny. Damn! Soulja. I thought maybe we going to do this cutthroat shit when I give this life back. I talked to Rell. He said he was going to handle that shit. But he got to be careful, because niggas damn near finished him. Well, hopefully, when I get up here, some motherfucker would help me get this time back. RIP, Soulja Slim.

Len

I sat on the porch in the project, smoking on some weed and loaded on some pills, thinking about Slim. I don't want to go to the funeral. It was too hard for me. I don't care if we was fucking no more. I was still in love with that nigga. Damn! Slim, you let them nigga get you like that. I guess any nigga can be got in the city. And them scare ass nigga that was with you ain't even do shit. The city is still doing them. The world still spinning, then I heard Rell ran down on one of them niggas out the seven ward and killed him at the gas station on Claiborne. I guess they still got real niggas out here. R.I.P., Slim.

The End

Lock Down Publications and Ca$h Presents assisted publishing packages.

BASIC PACKAGE $499

Editing

Cover Design

Formatting

UPGRADED PACKAGE $800

Typing

Editing

Cover Design

Formatting

ADVANCE PACKAGE $1,200

Typing

Editing

Cover Design

Formatting

Copyright registration

Proofreading

Upload book to Amazon

Robert Baptiste

LDP SUPREME PACKAGE $1,500

Typing

Editing

Cover Design

Formatting

Copyright registration

Proofreading

Set up Amazon account

Upload book to Amazon

Advertise on LDP Amazon and Facebook page

***Other services available upon request. Additional charges may apply

Lock Down Publications

P.O. Box 944

Stockbridge, GA 30281-9998

Phone # 470 303-9761

Submission Guideline

Submit the first three chapters of your completed manuscript to ldpsubmissions@gmail.com, subject line: Your book's title. The manuscript must be in a .doc file and sent as an attachment. Document should be in Times New Roman, double spaced and in size 12 font. Also, provide your synopsis and full contact information. If sending multiple submissions, they must each be in a separate email.

Have a story but no way to send it electronically? You can still submit to LDP/Ca$h Presents. Send in the first three chapters, written or typed, of your completed manuscript to:

**LDP: Submissions Dept
Po Box 944
Stockbridge, Ga 30281**

DO NOT send original manuscript. Must be a duplicate.

Provide your synopsis and a cover letter containing your full contact information.

Thanks for considering LDP and Ca$h Presents.

NEW RELEASES

PROTÉGÉ OF A LEGEND 2 by COREY ROBINSON

BRONX SAVAGES by ROMELL TUKES

A GANGSTA'S PAIN 3 by J-BLUNT

THE STREETS NEVER LET GO 3 by ROBERT BAPTISTE

The Streets Never Let Go 3

Coming Soon from Lock Down Publications/Ca$h Presents

BLOOD OF A BOSS **VI**

SHADOWS OF THE GAME II

TRAP BASTARD II

By **Askari**

LOYAL TO THE GAME **IV**

By **T.J. & Jelissa**

TRUE SAVAGE **VIII**

MIDNIGHT CARTEL IV

DOPE BOY MAGIC IV

CITY OF KINGZ III

NIGHTMARE ON SILENT AVE II

THE PLUG OF LIL MEXICO II

CLASSIC CITY II

By **Chris Green**

BLAST FOR ME **III**

A SAVAGE DOPEBOY III

CUTTHROAT MAFIA III

DUFFLE BAG CARTEL VII

HEARTLESS GOON VI

By **Ghost**

A HUSTLER'S DECEIT III

KILL ZONE II

BAE BELONGS TO ME III

TIL DEATH II

By **Aryanna**

KING OF THE TRAP III

By **T.J. Edwards**

GORILLAZ IN THE BAY V

3X KRAZY III

Robert Baptiste
STRAIGHT BEAST MODE III

De'Kari
KINGPIN KILLAZ IV
STREET KINGS III
PAID IN BLOOD III
CARTEL KILLAZ IV
DOPE GODS III

Hood Rich
SINS OF A HUSTLA II

ASAD
YAYO V
Bred In The Game 2

S. Allen
THE STREETS WILL TALK II

By Yolanda Moore
SON OF A DOPE FIEND III
HEAVEN GOT A GHETTO II
SKI MASK MONEY II

By Renta
LOYALTY AIN'T PROMISED III

By Keith Williams
I'M NOTHING WITHOUT HIS LOVE II
SINS OF A THUG II
TO THE THUG I LOVED BEFORE II
IN A HUSTLER I TRUST II

By Monet Dragun
QUIET MONEY IV
EXTENDED CLIP III
THUG LIFE IV

By **Trai'Quan**
THE STREETS MADE ME IV

The Streets Never Let Go 3
By **Larry D. Wright**
IF YOU CROSS ME ONCE III
ANGEL V
By **Anthony Fields**
THE STREETS WILL NEVER CLOSE IV
By **K'ajji**
HARD AND RUTHLESS III
KILLA KOUNTY IV
By **Khufu**
MONEY GAME III
By **Smoove Dolla**
JACK BOYS VS DOPE BOYS IV
A GANGSTA'S QUR'AN V
COKE GIRLZ II
COKE BOYS II
LIFE OF A SAVAGE V
CHI'RAQ GANGSTAS V
SOSA GANG II
BRONX SAVAGES II
By **Romell Tukes**
MURDA WAS THE CASE III
Elijah R. Freeman
AN UNFORESEEN LOVE IV
BABY, I'M WINTERTIME COLD III
By **Meesha**

QUEEN OF THE ZOO III
By **Black Migo**
CONFESSIONS OF A JACKBOY III
By **Nicholas Lock**

Robert Baptiste
GRIMEY WAYS III
By Ray Vinci
KING KILLA II
By Vincent "Vitto" Holloway
BETRAYAL OF A THUG III
By Fre$h
THE MURDER QUEENS III
By Michael Gallon
THE BIRTH OF A GANGSTER III
By Delmont Player
TREAL LOVE II
By Le'Monica Jackson
FOR THE LOVE OF BLOOD III
By Jamel Mitchell
RAN OFF ON DA PLUG II
By Paper Boi Rari
HOOD CONSIGLIERE III
By Keese
PRETTY GIRLS DO NASTY THINGS II
By Nicole Goosby
PROTÉGÉ OF A LEGEND III
By Corey Robinson
IT'S JUST ME AND YOU II
By Ah'Million
BORN IN THE GRAVE III
By Self Made Tay
FOREVER GANGSTA III
By Adrian Dulan
GORILLAZ IN THE TRENCHES II
By SayNoMore
THE COCAINE PRINCESS VII

The Streets Never Let Go 3
By King Rio
CRIME BOSS II
Playa Ray
LOYALTY IS EVERYTHING III
Molotti
HERE TODAY GONE TOMORROW II
By Fly Rock
REAL G'S MOVE IN SILENCE II
By Von Diesel

<u>**Available Now**</u>

RESTRAINING ORDER **I & II**
By **CA$H & Coffee**
LOVE KNOWS NO BOUNDARIES **I II & III**
By **Coffee**
RAISED AS A GOON I, II, III & IV
BRED BY THE SLUMS I, II, III
BLAST FOR ME I & II
ROTTEN TO THE CORE I II III
A BRONX TALE I, II, III
DUFFLE BAG CARTEL I II III IV V VI
HEARTLESS GOON I II III IV V
A SAVAGE DOPEBOY I II
DRUG LORDS I II III
CUTTHROAT MAFIA I II
KING OF THE TRENCHES

Robert Baptiste

By **Ghost**

LAY IT DOWN **I & II**

LAST OF A DYING BREED I II

BLOOD STAINS OF A SHOTTA I & II III

By **Jamaica**

LOYAL TO THE GAME I II III

LIFE OF SIN I, II III

By **TJ & Jelissa**

BLOODY COMMAS I & II

SKI MASK CARTEL I II & III

KING OF NEW YORK I II,III IV V

RISE TO POWER I II III

COKE KINGS I II III IV V

BORN HEARTLESS I II III IV

KING OF THE TRAP I II

By **T.J. Edwards**

IF LOVING HIM IS WRONG…I & II

LOVE ME EVEN WHEN IT HURTS I II III

By **Jelissa**

WHEN THE STREETS CLAP BACK I & II III

THE HEART OF A SAVAGE I II III IV

MONEY MAFIA I II

LOYAL TO THE SOIL I II III

By **Jibril Williams**

A DISTINGUISHED THUG STOLE MY HEART I II & III

LOVE SHOULDN'T HURT I II III IV

RENEGADE BOYS I II III IV

PAID IN KARMA I II III

SAVAGE STORMS I II III

AN UNFORESEEN LOVE I II III

BABY, I'M WINTERTIME COLD I II

The Streets Never Let Go 3

By **Meesha**

A GANGSTER'S CODE I &, II III

A GANGSTER'S SYN I II III

THE SAVAGE LIFE I II III

CHAINED TO THE STREETS I II III

BLOOD ON THE MONEY I II III

A GANGSTA'S PAIN I II III

By **J-Blunt**

PUSH IT TO THE LIMIT

By **Bre' Hayes**

BLOOD OF A BOSS **I, II, III, IV, V**

SHADOWS OF THE GAME

TRAP BASTARD

By **Askari**

THE STREETS BLEED MURDER **I, II & III**

THE HEART OF A GANGSTA I II& III

By **Jerry Jackson**

CUM FOR ME I II III IV V VI VII VIII

An **LDP Erotica Collaboration**

BRIDE OF A HUSTLA **I II & II**

THE FETTI GIRLS **I, II& III**

CORRUPTED BY A GANGSTA I, II III, IV

BLINDED BY HIS LOVE

THE PRICE YOU PAY FOR LOVE I, II ,III

DOPE GIRL MAGIC I II III

By **Destiny Skai**

WHEN A GOOD GIRL GOES BAD

By **Adrienne**

THE COST OF LOYALTY I II III

By **Kweli**

Robert Baptiste
A GANGSTER'S REVENGE **I II III & IV**
THE BOSS MAN'S DAUGHTERS I II III IV V
A SAVAGE LOVE **I & II**
BAE BELONGS TO ME I II
A HUSTLER'S DECEIT I, II, III
WHAT BAD BITCHES DO I, II, III
SOUL OF A MONSTER I II III
KILL ZONE
A DOPE BOY'S QUEEN I II III
TIL DEATH

By **Aryanna**
A KINGPIN'S AMBITON
A KINGPIN'S AMBITION **II**
I MURDER FOR THE DOUGH

By **Ambitious**
TRUE SAVAGE I II III IV V VI VII
DOPE BOY MAGIC I, II, III
MIDNIGHT CARTEL I II III
CITY OF KINGZ I II
NIGHTMARE ON SILENT AVE
THE PLUG OF LIL MEXICO II
CLASSIC CITY

By **Chris Green**
A DOPEBOY'S PRAYER

By **Eddie "Wolf" Lee**
THE KING CARTEL **I, II & III**

By **Frank Gresham**
THESE NIGGAS AIN'T LOYAL **I, II & III**

By **Nikki Tee**
GANGSTA SHYT **I II &III**

By **CATO**

The Streets Never Let Go 3
THE ULTIMATE BETRAYAL
By **Phoenix**
BOSS'N UP **I , II & III**
By **Royal Nicole**
I LOVE YOU TO DEATH
By **Destiny J**
I RIDE FOR MY HITTA
I STILL RIDE FOR MY HITTA
By **Misty Holt**
LOVE & CHASIN' PAPER
By **Qay Crockett**
TO DIE IN VAIN
SINS OF A HUSTLA
By **ASAD**
BROOKLYN HUSTLAZ
By **Boogsy Morina**
BROOKLYN ON LOCK I & II
By **Sonovia**
GANGSTA CITY
By **Teddy Duke**
A DRUG KING AND HIS DIAMOND I & II III
A DOPEMAN'S RICHES
HER MAN, MINE'S TOO I, II
CASH MONEY HO'S
THE WIFEY I USED TO BE I II
PRETTY GIRLS DO NASTY THINGS
By **Nicole Goosby**
TRAPHOUSE KING **I II & III**
KINGPIN KILLAZ I II III
STREET KINGS I II

Robert Baptiste
PAID IN BLOOD **I II**
CARTEL KILLAZ I II III
DOPE GODS I II
By **Hood Rich**
LIPSTICK KILLAH **I, II, III**
CRIME OF PASSION I II & III
FRIEND OR FOE I II III
By **Mimi**
STEADY MOBBN' **I, II, III**
THE STREETS STAINED MY SOUL I II III
By **Marcellus Allen**
WHO SHOT YA **I, II, III**
SON OF A DOPE FIEND I II
HEAVEN GOT A GHETTO
SKI MASK MONEY
Renta
GORILLAZ IN THE BAY **I II III IV**
TEARS OF A GANGSTA I II
3X KRAZY I II
STRAIGHT BEAST MODE I II
DE'KARI
TRIGGADALE I II III
MURDAROBER WAS THE CASE I II
Elijah R. Freeman
GOD BLESS THE TRAPPERS I, II, III
THESE SCANDALOUS STREETS I, II, III
FEAR MY GANGSTA I, II, III IV, V
THESE STREETS DON'T LOVE NOBODY I, II
BURY ME A G I, II, III, IV, V
A GANGSTA'S EMPIRE I, II, III, IV
THE DOPEMAN'S BODYGAURD I II

The Streets Never Let Go 3

THE REALEST KILLAZ I II III
THE LAST OF THE OGS I II III
Tranay Adams
THE STREETS ARE CALLING
Duquie Wilson
MARRIED TO A BOSS I II III
By Destiny Skai & Chris Green
KINGZ OF THE GAME I II III IV V VI
CRIME BOSS
Playa Ray
SLAUGHTER GANG I II III
RUTHLESS HEART I II III
By Willie Slaughter
FUK SHYT
By Blakk Diamond
DON'T F#CK WITH MY HEART I II
By Linnea
ADDICTED TO THE DRAMA I II III
IN THE ARM OF HIS BOSS II
By Jamila
YAYO I II III IV
A SHOOTER'S AMBITION I II
BRED IN THE GAME
By S. Allen
TRAP GOD I II III
RICH $AVAGE I II III
MONEY IN THE GRAVE I II III
By Martell Troublesome Bolden
FOREVER GANGSTA I II
GLOCKS ON SATIN SHEETS I II

Robert Baptiste

By Adrian Dulan

TOE TAGZ I II III IV

LEVELS TO THIS SHYT I II

IT'S JUST ME AND YOU

By Ah'Million

KINGPIN DREAMS I II III

RAN OFF ON DA PLUG

By Paper Boi Rari

CONFESSIONS OF A GANGSTA I II III IV

CONFESSIONS OF A JACKBOY I II

By Nicholas Lock

I'M NOTHING WITHOUT HIS LOVE

SINS OF A THUG

TO THE THUG I LOVED BEFORE

A GANGSTA SAVED XMAS

IN A HUSTLER I TRUST

By Monet Dragun

CAUGHT UP IN THE LIFE I II III

THE STREETS NEVER LET GO I II III

By Robert Baptiste

NEW TO THE GAME I II III

MONEY, MURDER & MEMORIES I II III

By **Malik D. Rice**

LIFE OF A SAVAGE I II III IV

A GANGSTA'S QUR'AN I II III IV

MURDA SEASON I II III

GANGLAND CARTEL I II III

CHI'RAQ GANGSTAS I II III IV

KILLERS ON ELM STREET I II III

JACK BOYZ N DA BRONX I II III

A DOPEBOY'S DREAM I II III

The Streets Never Let Go 3
JACK BOYS VS DOPE BOYS I II III
COKE GIRLZ
COKE BOYS
SOSA GANG
BRONX SAVAGES
By Romell Tukes
LOYALTY AIN'T PROMISED I II
By Keith Williams
QUIET MONEY I II III
THUG LIFE I II III
EXTENDED CLIP I II
A GANGSTA'S PARADISE
By **Trai'Quan**
THE STREETS MADE ME I II III
By **Larry D. Wright**
THE ULTIMATE SACRIFICE I, II, III, IV, V, VI
KHADIFI
IF YOU CROSS ME ONCE I II
ANGEL I II III IV
IN THE BLINK OF AN EYE
By **Anthony Fields**
THE LIFE OF A HOOD STAR
By Ca$h & Rashia Wilson
THE STREETS WILL NEVER CLOSE I II III
By K'ajji
CREAM I II III
THE STREETS WILL TALK
By Yolanda Moore
NIGHTMARES OF A HUSTLA I II III
By King Dream

Robert Baptiste
CONCRETE KILLA I II III
VICIOUS LOYALTY I II III
By Kingpen
HARD AND RUTHLESS I II
MOB TOWN 251
THE BILLIONAIRE BENTLEYS I II III
REAL G'S MOVE IN SILENCE
By Von Diesel
GHOST MOB
Stilloan Robinson
MOB TIES I II III IV V VI
SOUL OF A HUSTLER, HEART OF A KILLER I II
GORILLAZ IN THE TRENCHES
By SayNoMore
BODYMORE MURDERLAND I II III
THE BIRTH OF A GANGSTER I II
By Delmont Player
FOR THE LOVE OF A BOSS
By C. D. Blue
MOBBED UP I II III IV
THE BRICK MAN I II III IV V
THE COCAINE PRINCESS I II III IV V VI
By King Rio
KILLA KOUNTY I II III IV
By Khufu
MONEY GAME I II
By Smoove Dolla
A GANGSTA'S KARMA I II III
By FLAME
KING OF THE TRENCHES I II III
by **GHOST & TRANAY ADAMS**

The Streets Never Let Go 3

QUEEN OF THE ZOO I II
By **Black Migo**
GRIMEY WAYS I II
By Ray Vinci
XMAS WITH AN ATL SHOOTER
By Ca$h & Destiny Skai
KING KILLA
By Vincent "Vitto" Holloway
BETRAYAL OF A THUG I II
By Fre$h
THE MURDER QUEENS I II
By Michael Gallon
TREAL LOVE
By Le'Monica Jackson
FOR THE LOVE OF BLOOD I II
By Jamel Mitchell
HOOD CONSIGLIERE I II
By Keese
PROTÉGÉ OF A LEGEND I II
By Corey Robinson
BORN IN THE GRAVE I II
By Self Made Tay
MOAN IN MY MOUTH
By XTASY
TORN BETWEEN A GANGSTER AND A GENTLEMAN
By J-BLUNT & Miss Kim
LOYALTY IS EVERYTHING I II
Molotti
HERE TODAY GONE TOMORROW
By Fly Rock

Robert Baptiste
PILLOW PRINCESS
By S. Hawkins

BOOKS BY LDP'S CEO, CA$H

TRUST IN NO MAN
TRUST IN NO MAN 2
TRUST IN NO MAN 3
BONDED BY BLOOD
SHORTY GOT A THUG
THUGS CRY
THUGS CRY 2
THUGS CRY 3
TRUST NO BITCH
TRUST NO BITCH 2
TRUST NO BITCH 3
TIL MY CASKET DROPS
RESTRAINING ORDER
RESTRAINING ORDER 2
IN LOVE WITH A CONVICT
LIFE OF A HOOD STAR
XMAS WITH AN ATL SHOOTER

Robert Baptiste

WITHDRAWN

CPSIA information can be obtained
at www.ICGtesting.com
Printed in the USA
LVHW041837240223
740361LV00001B/136